Holding Faith

Holding Faith

Kelly Aul

Scripture quotations are from the King James Version of the Bible

Printed in the United States of America

ISBN   978-0692212622

Purebooks artwork by Jessica Benson

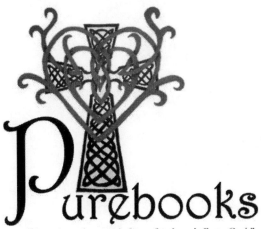

"Blessed are the pure in heart for they shall see God."
Matthew 5:8

Dress made by Matti's Millinery & Costumes

Making Your Costume Dreams Come True!
www.mattionline.com

BOOKS *by* KELLY AUL

NEVER FORSAKEN

1. Audrey's Sunrise
2. In the Midst of Darkness
3. Holding Faith
4. Everlasting

RELENTLESS

1. Unspoken Pursuit

Special thanks to:

- ❖ My family. Your help, encouragement, support, excitement, and love mean so much to me. It is something I will never forget.

- ❖ To my mom, Maggie Aul, and sister, Natalie Aul, thank you so much for your amazing editing help.

- ❖ To Hannah Wagner and Matti Wangerin, thank you for another stunning dress for the cover. The Never Forsaken books wouldn't be the same without Matti's Millinery & Costumes.

Most importantly, I give all the glory to my Heavenly Father, my Lord and Savior, Jesus Christ, and the precious leading of the Holy Spirit.

I dedicate this book
to my readers, who have been so faithful to
Audrey's Sunrise and have turned it into
The Never Forsaken series!

"Holding faith, and a good conscience; which some having put away concerning faith have made shipwreck."

1 Timothy 1:19

PART I

CHAPTER ONE

London, England   *June 1844*

"Captain, Miss Hephzibah is here for you." Weston turned to look over the rail and saw his sister standing at the bottom of the gangplank, trying to stay out of the way of the sailor's loading and unloading. She held a dish, carefully wrapped under her arm.

Most likely filled with goodies of some sort, he thought. "Thank you, Samuel. Here, take over for me," he handed the inventory papers over to the sailor and walked down to her.

"Hephzibah, glad to see ya. We arrived only moments ago."

"Aye, I saw the sails o' The chuffin' Mighty Hester from my winda. I brought theur sum wee cakes," she handed the dish to Weston.

"Thank you. I hope you haven't outdone yourself."

"Noa, no…I had ta come down and see ya."

"Everything alright?"

"Theur worry abaht me too much. I come and welcome ya every time ya come home."

"Alright…maybe I do. I think about you often, Sister. Your certain nothin' is wrong?" he asked once more just to be sure.

"Well, surely I become lonely once in eur while and miss cookin' fo ya…." When she saw Weston swiftly open his mouth to protest to tell her for the hundredth time the reason why she didn't cook any longer, Hephzibah stopped him by raising her hand. "I kna it's not ter be anymore but theur mussn't worry…for greyta is He that is in me. I'm fine and dandy."

"Your words are convincing. I'll try my best not to."

"Gran'…I've come ta welcome you, sa now ahl leave theur to thy fettle. Enjoy the treaties."

"Thanks again. I will see ya later tonight," Weston waved as Hephzibah turned to leave.

"Hello, Miss Hephzibah." As she walked down the gangplank, a sailor passed and greeted kindly.

"Why 'ello Rob, how are ya fairin'?"

"Oh, well enough. Sure do miss you though."

"Aye…you and the lovely food you used to make!" Another sailor must have overheard and shouted from his place on the deck. The act made Hephzibah chuckle.

"That's right gran' of you ta say, but I'm sure Nelson is a fine cook," she shouted back.

"His food is lousy in comparison." Hephzibah was about to reply when yet another shout was heard, this time from the cook himself!

"'ey! Ya know I can hear ya!"

"Well, it's bloody true, isn't it?" the sailor came back at him. Everyone within earshot of the group joined in the laughter.

"I'd betta nip on. Mind yourself, Rob."

"Take care, Miss."

Hephzibah was humming a cheerful tune as she strolled to the market, looking at the different ships, equipment, and cargo on The Port along the way. About one block in front of her, she noticed three men leaning against a well-worn building. They were all watching something very intently and whispering to each other seriously. Hephzibah's pace immediately quickened, along with her heart beat, as flash backs filled with sad memories came to her mind. For some reason she glanced at them as she passed by and recognized one of them.

"Dorcet...." she blurted out the name that came to mind, but couldn't think of the young man's first name right away. The moment Hephzibah stopped, the other two men with him strolled down the street a ways, however, not before giving the young man a strange but stern look. After watching the exchange, Hephzibah glanced at the young man again. She took in his brown hair, unshorn dirty face, and rugged clothes. It wasn't until she looked at his eyes and saw his rebellious, angry state and the way he set his jaw firmly in stubbornness when she remembered.

"Oh, that's right...Edwin Dorcet." Edwin seemed annoyed by her presence, especially when he saw who it was.

What does this nosey old lady want? Edwin glanced at the other men who were waiting for him to get rid of the unwanted company. *She better not ruin this for me!* He had much at stake with his newest business partners.

"What are ya doin' all the way up 'ere? Sa far away from Morrison's? I hope nuffin' went wrong wif theur working for him...you, your brother, and father?"

"No," Edwin sighed heavily. *I don't have to explain myself to her.* "They still work there."

"'ow come ya don't anymore?" Edwin shifted back and forth and gazed down the street again. He could tell his consort's patience was growing thin. They surely wouldn't wait long.

"Just cause...I found something better." With that, he turned to leave.

"Edwin," Hephzibah gently caught his arm which made his gaze jerk back to her. He looked at her hand on his arm as if revolted by it. His anger seemed to spark by the simple act. "You don't have ta be wif that riffraff. You're betta than their kind." Hephzibah watched his face reddin in fury as he ripped his arm from her grip and stormed off.

No one tells me what to do, he thought.

Hephzibah could only watch him walk away, knowing all too well it would only end in misery for the young man.

Lord, I pray he will come to himself and You before it's too late.

CHAPTER TWO

s soon as the last song had been sung and the house lights brightened a bit, Rylan glanced over at Brenna and found her beaming.

"What a wonderful performance!" Brenna soon met his gaze and exclaimed.

"It was rather entertaining tonight."

"As opposed to other times when it hasn't been?"

"Well…I suppose." Rylan stood along with everyone else in the packed building and offered his arm to escort her out of the theatre. He had gone to countless operas before this one and found them rather dull, or so he thought, until he attended with Brenna, Scarlette Kinsey and also Scarlette's escort, Daniel Eldridge. He'd never had so much fun being with the two cheerful, giddy, and winsome sisters. Just merely watching them enjoy the evening brought a smile to his face. They didn't have any hidden motives, competing with each other in gaining the most attention. They were lighthearted and jovial about everything they did and were never hard to please. Rylan was a bit reluctant to see the evening come to an end. Unbeknownst to him was how close Brenna was to declining he and David's invitation upon first hearing about it. She was still a bit nervous in wondering if Rylan would accidentally reveal her secret or not. If it wasn't for Scarlette, who badly wished to go to the opera, Brenna would have never considered accepting. She was so glad she finally gave in for it had proved to be very enjoyable. She was also relieved that Rylan seemed to have dismissed the entire ordeal Brenna was afraid of.

"Did you two fancy the opera as much as we did?" Rylan called to Daniel and Scarlette, who exited the row first.

"Very much," Daniel answered.

"I especially liked their gorgeous, glittering costumes. Brenna, what would it be like to wear such a thing as the main performer? Not to mention the wigs and cosmetics," Scarlette stated dreamily.

"It would be fun, perhaps for a time."

The foursome patiently weaved their way out of The Theatre Royal and onto the street. Daniel and Scarlette took the lead and strolled arm in arm to the carriage while Rylan and Brenna followed. Rylan kept the pace as slow as possible, cherishing his last few moments with Miss Kinsey.

"Well, if it isn't Lord Quenell." Rylan immediately knew who the sarcastic voice belonged to and cringed.

"Please don't stop or pay him any mind. He means no harm," Rylan quickly whispered when Brenna was going to stop to see who it was. He hoped he spoke the truth.

"Hey paddy, are you too good to stop and speak to me or do you only keep company with your kind now?"

Daniel was just helping Scarlette climb into the carriage when he heard the commotion. When he turned to see what was going on, he saw Rylan and Brenna coming towards him and three men taunting them from behind. When the couple wouldn't acknowledge them, one of the men moved in front of them, forcing the couple to come to a stop.

"Oh, that's right…maybe you can't understand me," he then spoke in a sloppy Irish accent and shouted in Rylan's face, "Do ya tink yisser family is better than al' av us? Yet you're 'ere. Ya don't belong 'ere. Go back ter your own bog-trottin' kind! There…is that better?" Rylan remained calm and stood unmoving, looking straight ahead. He felt Brenna grasp his arm tighter.

"Carter, leave them alone!" Daniel approached after telling Scarlette to stay put, Daniel approached.

"What are you doing with him and this skirt?" Carter turned to him and insulted Brenna.

"Stop…not here," Daniel tried to reason quietly to not cause a commotion on the crowded street. Because it seemed this wouldn't end quickly, Daniel neared Brenna's side. "Miss Kinsey, you had better go to your sister." Brenna finally released Rylan's arm and moved away. The three men were still blurting out spiteful jeering's, but Rylan would not pay them any mind.

Brenna did move toward the carriage, although she couldn't make herself leave completely. She was curious about what these men were speaking of.

What is going on? She tried to figure it out and stopped to watch at a safe distance.

Daniel Eldridge set his gaze on the instigator of the group and swiftly covered the distance between them as if taking control of the situation. He put himself in front of Rylan, only inches from Carter's face.

"You need to leave before this goes any further. Otherwise, I will call the constables."

"Oh really?" Carter sneered, "You know just as well as I that the only person who would interest them is your pathetic friend here."

"He's nothing better than a mick."

"The police know filth just by the look of you." The other two trouble makers joined in and shouted other unspeakable profanity.

What are they referring to? Lord Quenell is an upstanding gentleman...isn't he? Brenna felt helpless.

One of the men roughly shoved Rylan from behind nearly sending him to the ground. Even after regaining his composure, he still would not consent to their treatment.

"Come on! Take a swing! One swing is all it would take to send you to the lockup," Carter laughed and was joined by the other men.

Brenna watched people pass by on the street. For a moment they appeared concerned, but when they would slow to get a better look at the men involved, they would move on in a hurry.

Because Rylan ignored the harassment and kept his gaze on the ground, the men finally tired of their efforts.

"Well, since this so called earl isn't man enough to stand up for himself...let's go," Carter past Daniel by colliding into his shoulder then glared at Rylan. It wasn't until he was right next to Rylan that Carter spat in his face and left. Even then, Rylan held his repose.

Brenna watched the three men saunter down the street then moved her gaze back to Rylan and Daniel, who slowly moved toward her. Rylan calmly reached inside his dress-coat for a handkerchief and began to wipe his face. Part of her wondered why he hadn't stood up for himself, yet at the same time she admired him for his resolve in the midst of pressure. Brenna didn't quite know what to say, for Rylan seemed a little embarrassed in knowing she had witnessed the ordeal.

"No harm done," he said quickly when Brenna was about to ask if he was alright. That was all they said for some time. In truth, because Rylan knew what Brenna had heard, he didn't know what to say.

I don't want her to think I'm a criminal of some kind! Yet, could she accept it if I told her everything? He questioned himself as they all climbed inside and were off. *I must be honest. I'll only answer any questions she might have. I can do nothing more than the truth,* he finally settled and was relieved when Brenna didn't say anything more about it for the rest of the evening. The foursome managed to keep the conversation light.

After Scarlette and Brenna were dropped off at the Cheverell's and had said their goodbyes to Daniel and Rylan, Brenna had much to think on. Though she had many unanswered questions about Lord Quenell's controversial encounter, one thing stood out from all else. It was the way Rylan had acted through it. His peaceful state and refusal to fight made a substantial impression on her. Brenna's already high regard for Rylan had greatly increased that evening, along with something else. The feelings she was beginning to have for him confused her.

"Lord, what is it?" Brenna whispered the moment her head hit the pillow. She prayed for several minutes and found that one particular question kept coming to mind before she fell asleep.

"Does Rylan believe in You? He said he read from The Bible daily…but does he love You as I do?"

"And God said, Let there be light: and there was light. And God saw the light, that it was good: and God divided the light from the darkness."

Genesis 1:3~4

CHAPTER THREE

Primrose ~ Augustine, England   *July 1844*

"You may kiss the bride. I now present to you Mr. and Mrs. Jacob Harper." Everyone present at the quaint wedding, held in the garden, clapped and cheered. As soon as everyone gave the newest wedded couple their congratulations, they moved to the lovely luncheon, also set up in Audrey's favorite place behind Primrose.

Audrey couldn't get over seeing how happy her mother was. When Rose and Jake first announced their engagement it came as a shock to the entire family. However, those closest to them were beginning to catch on to their growing affection toward each other for quite some time. The sheer joy that radiated from them confirmed it to be a good match and put Audrey at ease. They were both faithful Christians and that was the best part about it in her mind.

"Oh, mother, I'm so happy for you!" Audrey embraced Rose when it was her and Joseph's turn to congratulate the couple.

"Thank you." Tears brimmed in both women's eyes. While they spoke further, Joseph shook Jake's hand.

"Congratulations, Jake. I knew somethin' wus up witcha two…but didn't nu you had it in ya. It sort of makes us family nigh, though it feels loike we 'av been for years."

"I couldn't agree with you more," Jake's grin never left his face.

"Well, we had better move on to our other guests," Rose mentioned. Jake took her arm and they left. Audrey carefully scanned the small crowd for her dear friend. She was aching to go to Lanna the minute she saw her sit towards the back with her family. She would have gone to her straight away but the ceremony was just starting. It wasn't hard to find Lanna's large family.

Lanna felt the same for when they caught each other's eye at that moment, they eagerly made their way to one another.

"Oh Lanna, how I've missed you!" They embraced and nearly cried with joy.

"It 'as been so long," Lanna choked. Both of their families had no choice but to follow them. Every member had heard so much about the other family that they were curious to finally put the faces to the names.

"Let me look at your bonnie family!" Lanna gently pulled away when she realized the precious baby Audrey held.

"This is Kalin and this is Evan," Audrey turned to her son, who held onto Joseph's hand, and playfully ruffled his hair.

"How wonderful! He looks just like his owl lad. Hello Joseph, it's grand to see you," Lanna said and Joseph nodded. She then stepped to the side to introduce her dear ones.

"This is Tully and baby Audrey, though she's not such a baby anymore. Then you remember my husband Stephen, Katherine, Phillip, Andrew, and Stephen Jr.. Scarlette and Brenna are currently in London for the Season."

"I do remember them, though it has been quite some time. You've all grown up so much!" Audrey exclaimed then bent down to Lanna's two children whom she hadn't met yet. The last time Lanna and Audrey had been together was for her and Joseph's wedding. "You two are simply adorable. Shall we go and take a seat at the tables over there? Perhaps we can push two together so we can all fit." When everyone agreed, they slowly made their way to be seated. On their way, Rose and Jake stopped to talk to Lanna and her family so Audrey and Joseph continued over to the tables to give them a moment alone.

"Evan, please come away from the cake. We must wait for everyone," Audrey spied her son going towards the special desert. Joseph was made aware also.

"Evan, cum 'ere, lad," he crouched down and stretched his arms out to the three years old. Evan, named after Audrey's beloved father, needed no other persuasion and happily ran to his father. "There's me boy," Joseph lifted him up quickly in a sweeping motion, causing him to giggle.

"Let's have a seat at the table over there and pull over the one beside it, shall we?" Audrey gathered her pastel skirt in one hand and held the baby in the other as she led the way.

It wasn't long after getting settled that Audrey noticed the wistful look on her husband's face. It was the same poignant expression he wore shortly after meeting his new daughter, Kalin, only four months earlier. When she noticed it then, she asked him about it. His reply held some merit. He said that having a little girl and a family of his own, was causing him to think more about his own family and what might have become of them. Audrey figured it was the same reason now at the wedding. Deep down, she knew it always sort of bothered Joseph that, while she was surrounded by her family at their wedding, his could never be there.

Audrey grasped Joseph's hand lovingly and silently prayed for him.

CHAPTER FOUR

*J*t was nearly a week since the night of the opera and Rylan had thought and prayed a lot ever since. Because of his growing affection toward Brenna, he wanted to make sure he was doing the right concerning her. The last thing he wanted to do was scare her away.

He finally got the answer to what he'd been seeking a few days later. Rylan now knew that if he truly cared for Miss Kinsey, he should tell her more about himself or at least explain what Carter had said.

When he first gained enough courage to face Brenna, he had gone to the Cheverell's home two days earlier in hopes of getting a chance to speak with her. However, when he'd come upon the house he saw two young men being let inside by the butler. He knew well that during the time following their official coming out into society, Scarlette and Brenna would receive callers until the Season ended. In seeing the gentlemen callers, Rylan began to doubt his plan and swiftly grew embarrassed from the humbling previous events. His hesitation caused his newly found bravery to vanish. He left just as quickly as he'd come. His chance to see Brenna wouldn't present itself again until some days later at the home of the Wakefield's. It was a private ball so Rylan wasn't certain if Brenna would even be there. But something told him otherwise.

He caught sight of Brenna and her family while dancing with an old family friend. Brenna, Scarlette, and the Cheverell's were mingling on the outskirts of the ballroom.

They must have just arrived. How did I miss seeing them come in? Rylan strained to see where they were slowly headed and hardly noticed the song had ended.

"Thank you for the dance. It was lovely."

"It was my pleasure," Rylan was instantly brought back to the present, looked down at his dance partner, and smiled.

"I hope I didn't slow you down with these old bones."

"You were just fine," Rylan tried to remain focused as he led her to her seat for he'd lost sight of Brenna, "We will most certainly have to dance again soon, I hope."

"Oh my dear boy, you are too kind. We will have to see." After taking a bow, Rylan was off to find Miss Kinsey. He located the rest of her family talking in a group next to some open doors that led to the veranda. He poked his head outside and found her alone.

Perfect! He strolled towards her and looked up at the stars in the clear sky.

"Beautiful night," he stopped just beside her, "I'm glad you chose to enjoy a bit of it."

"Oh, good evening," Brenna was pleased to see who it was and Rylan was equally as happy to see that she was.

"I haven't seen you for a few days. How have you been?" He wished he could skip the small talk and start explaining things straight away, but knew it would still take some leading up to.

"Quite busy."

"I'm sure you and your sister have countless callers taking up much of your time of late."

"Well, yes…that is…." Brenna didn't know how to answer. She wondered what he meant by such a comment. *Especially considering that he wasn't among them since going to the theatre,* she thought and tried to reply. "Perhaps not as many as you suggest." Unbeknown to her, Rylan had regretted his jealous sounding statement the moment he said it.

How foolish of me. Shape up man! he scolded himself.

"How have you been?" Brenna asked.

Where should I begin? Rylan asked himself, knowing this was his chance to speak to her while being somewhat alone. The doors to the noisy room were wide open behind them, but this was the only kind of alone that was allowed.

"I've given the night we attended the theatre a great deal of thought and would like to explain what happened on the street after the performance." Brenna saw him get rather nervous at the mention of that evening. As much as she wanted to know, she felt she should give him an out.

"I would like to understand, though, I won't feel badly if you can't."

"Thank you, but it's unfair to keep it from you. I don't know precisely where to begin." Rylan broke eye contact and looked out over the gardens, searching for guidance.

Brenna almost felt guilty in watching him struggle.

"First, I believe you need to know some things about my family. That is, if you haven't heard some things already. I know how gossip can travels." Brenna couldn't help but recall Cora's story. She felt ashamed for giving it too much thought in the last month.

"My parents and I live on an estate in Ireland, passed down through many generations. Many tenants cultivate the land we own. Sadly, not very many people treat Irish as kindly as my family does. My father stayed true to his word and with his help, twenty Irishmen were granted into parliament over forty years ago, much to the dismay of most. My family was rejected, especially from high society. My parents felt, and we still do at times, like reprobates. In fact, our estate and surrounding land are often vandalized. To further irritate everyone opposed, he married an Irish maid. Everyone thought it was only in efforts to further his cause. Of course it wasn't true. The attacks got more violent as time went on and my father was even shot. Years later, during one Season, my parents traveled to London for the sitting of parliament. In their absence someone burned nearly every one of our tenant's houses and fields, all but the estate itself. Upon their return, no one would speak to them…not even the Irish, who normally revered him as a hero. Everyone thought it was deliberate arson because it conveniently happened while they were away."

"That's horrible," Brenna finally stated. What she had seen of Rylan's parents now made much more sense. *They're still outcasts after all these years.*

"It almost broke my father during the court appearances but the most disheartening to him was knowing some of his tenants had lost their lives in the fires. I strongly believe he would never have made it, if not for his faith in God."

"What became of it?"

"I was some time later that evidence was finally found to prove he was innocent and the entire matter was then dropped. Though my father was found faultless, it did little to change anything else. The majority to this day still think my father was behind it. Because of all that, any little squabble over any sort of thing could very well mean prison for my family or I."

"So that's why the man from the other night wanted you to fight him," Brenna said quietly. She chided herself for believing any of the preposterous gossip to be true. Rylan nodded in return then turned from looking at the gardens to face Brenna.

"That brings me to something else." Brenna met his gaze. "It took me some time to figure it out, but I finally came to the conclusion with some help." A look of concern formed on Brenna's face that made Rylan not want to go on, yet he knew he must use this opportunity before they were interrupted like so many other times. "That night…when you and someone with you, were attacked…." Brenna immediately grew pale.

How does he know?

"I was there…I mean, I was the one who threw the rocks. And you were just a young girl…I brought you to safety," Rylan slowly explained. It left Brenna was dumbstruck. Along with countless questions, she felt numb as she tried to remember the young man who'd rescued her that night.

"How? Why did you disappear?" Brenna choked for she tried to speak as fast as the questions flashed through her mind.

"That's just it. Because my family is continuously scrutinized, I knew once my name was made known to the constable, he would no doubt think I was the attacker and…murderer." Brenna stepped back, trying to regain her thoughts. Rylan hoped he hadn't made a mistake by telling her in such a way, but there was no other way. He didn't follow her just yet.

"I'm sorry for everything you've had to go through."

"I just…hardly know what to think. Right when it seems I've gotten a grasp on things, everything is up in the air again," Brenna said.

"Might I ask what happened? I've wondered about it ever since," Rylan eventually asked and slowly approached. Brenna was relieved he changed the subject a bit. Fear tempted to rise up in her. She couldn't help but wonder if the mere mentioning of her past would awaken everything she'd finally been able to rid herself from.

Only with the Lord's help. She was swiftly reminded. *With the Lord I was freed from my past, and with the Lord, I will be able to speak of it without fear!* "To tell you fully, I would need to go back further than that night."

"Please do." It was what Rylan had wanted to know from the very beginning, but he didn't want to pressure her.

"I'll put it as briefly as possible. I have two older brothers. They locked me inside a trunk that was in the Boston harbor. The next thing I knew was being found among the cargo. Because the ship was already too far from land to turn back, I had to wait until we reached England before I could return. During the journey I was put in the care of a wonderfully odd woman. Her name was Hephzibah and she taught me many things in those three long months. We reached England and I went with her to the market. It was there…we were attacked. You see we weren't related yet she was very dear to me." Sorrow swiftly washed over her so she chose to move on instead of pondering over Hephzibah's death. Brenna's voice trembled as she sighed heavily. "Before you left, did you happen to see that Hephzibah had vanished? It was all so strange."

"What? Vanished?" He quickly wondered.

"I don't know how or who would have done it, but the constable was just as confused as I. He thought I was crazy and we'd made the whole thing up. I guess we'll never know. I was then brought to an orphanage." Guilt hit Rylan hard the moment he heard it.

What did you expect would happen when you left? Everyone knew orphanages are never, if very rarely, a pleasurable place. *Why did I leave? I'm nothing more than a coward.*

"I was adopted by the Kinsey's a few years later…and here I am."

"What of your family in Boston? Have you contacted them

of your whereabouts?"

"I sent them word over a year ago, but received nothing in return." Seemingly every day, Brenna wondered and desperately tried to come up with a good explanation as to why her family hadn't responded to her letter until she nearly went mad with worry over it. She was forced to resign herself to never seeing her family again. Her simple reply baffled Rylan and made him unable to except it.

"Is it because of some kind of hardship you know of that could be keeping them from replying?"

"No, nothing like that. My family is very well off. My father, William Dorcet owns a large bank. I was actually very spoiled because of it." Brenna wasn't prepared for what she was about to hear. Rylan was quickly becoming angry at her family. To him, there was no earthly reason why they wouldn't be searching everywhere for her.

"Well, it must be something!" His voice grew a little louder that Brenna glanced at the open door to see if anyone heard him.

"What do you mean?" She couldn't figure out why he was so upset. She lowered her voice in hopes to quiet him.

"There must be a reason…just thinking about how they could leave you like this, completely uncaring, angers me!"

"What do you— " Brenna was cut off as he continued.

"Why, if it was my daughter, I would stop at nothing…I would never stop searching if it was the last thing I did…no matter what!"

"What do you know of my family? You don't know them or me for that matter!" It was now Brenna's turn to raise her voice once he'd finished ranting. "You find out about my situation moments ago and you're already blaming my family, of whom you know nothing about in the least! Don't you think I've wondered the same…lying awake at night, trying to figure out why they haven't responded? Wondering if something happened to them or if they even care? No! You don't think of those things before going around making accusations!" Brenna started to leave so Rylan wouldn't see her angry tears fall.

"Wait, please come back," Rylan immediately went after her and grabbed the back of her arm in haste, a bit harder than he meant to. The act instantly brought Brenna back to her dreams, where the chilling presence reached for her from behind, right before pulling her into the darkness. She froze as her breath caught in her throat.

"Unhand me, sir," her cold formal tone made Ryan regret his impulsive move. He released her and watched her rush back into the ballroom and feared he might never see her again.

"Lord, what have I done?" he whispered.

CHAPTER FIVE

Gresham Detective Agency
Boston, Massachusetts

July 3, 1844
London, England

To Whom It May Concern,

I need to hire a Private Investigator to help in regards to a mystery of sorts. Unfortunately, all I know of the matter is that it concerns Willian Dorcet and his family. He supposedly owns a bank in Boston. His daughter, Miss Brenna Dorcet went missing some years ago. I know of her whereabouts and she has tried to contact her family to no avail. Please find out anything you can about it. Enclosed is a sincere appreciation for your efforts. I will send further means if needed, once I hear from you.

Thank you again,

Sincerely,

The Right Honourable Rylan Lennox, Earl of Guenell

Rylan sealed the envelope and gazed out the window from his writing desk. He hoped and prayed his mere effort to help Brenna would somehow act as an apology for his actions. He loathed what he had done and thought perhaps this might ease his conscience.

'Therefore if thou bring thy gift to the altar, and there rememberest that thy brother hath ought against thee; Leave

*there thy gift before the altar, and go thy way; first be
reconciled to thy brother, and then come and offer thy gift.'*

Rylan finished reading the verse in Matthew, closed his
Bible, and stood. Though he had known all along that it was
wrong to do nothing about his rash actions, what he'd just read
confirmed it.

Rylan walked to the front door before his mind could talk
him out of it.

*Lord, I'll do what you ask, no matter how humbling it may
be. All I hope is that she'll at least see me and hear me out,* he
silently prayed and descended the steps to the street. He would
enjoy a long walk to the Cheverell's for it would give him plenty
of time to think of how to begin his apology.

The Cheverell's home had just come into view when he
noticed a carriage sitting in front of the entrance.

*I hope it's not a caller. Oh...why must they be so persistent?
Don't they know the young ladies tire of their earnest and endless
pursuit?* Rylan slowed a bit as he got a little closer. It was then he
saw some people come outside. It wasn't gentlemen callers at all,
but the lord and lady of the house followed by Scarlette and
Brenna, and lastly two ladies maids. Rylan stopped for he didn't
want to intrude or so he told himself as an excuse to delay his
true reason in coming.

He watched from a safe distance to not be seen. Instead of
climbing into the carriage, the family began to hug each other as
if saying goodbye. It finally dawned in him what was going on
when two servants, holding a great deal of luggage, loaded the
back of the carriage. *They're leaving?* Part of him urged him
forward before it was too late, yet the other part caused him to
hesitate. Rylan helplessly watched as Scarlette and Brenna slowly
waved one last time to their aunt and uncle and quietly climbed
into the carriage.

"What's wrong?" Scarlette asked Brenna when she sighed heavily as soon as they were seated. "You thought he would come, didn't you?" Because Brenna's gaze was hidden from looking down, Scarlette reached over and lifted her sister's large hat to see she spoke the truth. Brenna certainly looked sad over something and it wasn't only from saying goodbye to Adelaide and Bertram. However, Scarlette didn't know what else to say to her. Sure they both came away from their first Season without getting engaged, but she knew it wasn't unusual for the first time, especially when they were both fairly young with plenty of time to find a husband. Something had happened at the last ball they'd attended, yet Brenna wouldn't speak of it, no matter how many times or different ways Scarlette tried to find out more. All she could tell was it had to do with Lord Quenell.

I can't tell her...not now. Not in front of Eleta and Pensee. Brenna thought. The carriage began to move down the street when, for no reason at all, Brenna glanced back at the Cheverell's one last time. As she did, she caught sight of a man standing on the side of the road. He did nothing but stand there, staring...at her! *It's Rylan! There's no question.* She wanted nothing more than to stop the driver, get out, and run to him to tell him how sorry she was, however, her stubbornness from childhood remained in her. As sorry as she was and as much as she thought she loved him, Brenna wouldn't allow herself to do anything about it. She knew very well she'd overreacted that night. Why, she shared the very thoughts Rylan had gotten upset over. She completely agreed with what Rylan had said about her family. What still concerned her was how the evening ended. How Rylan had taken her arm and the frightening look in his eye.

What if I'm overreacting about that as well? Oh, I don't know, Brenna sighed again, *Lord, was it all just an infatuation that he cared for me at all? That an earl actually loved someone like me?* Suddenly another thought came to her. *If he really wanted to stop and speak with me...if he truly loved me, he could have done something and easily stopped us from leaving. That's it then.* She did all she could not to cry in front of Scarlette and the ladies maids as they rounded the corner.

Rylan had to force himself to stay put as he longingly watched them leave, particularly when he saw Brenna turned back and looked at him. How he kicked himself for saying and acting the way he did that night, but it was too late. In the back of his mind he couldn't help but think perhaps this was for the best, at least for the time being. Because he had partially lost control when he'd reached for Brenna, it startled him a bit. That he could lose his composure so easily, bothered him to no end. He prided himself, perhaps more than he should have, for remaining calm and collected in all situations. His trust in the Lord of his life also wavered that night. It concerned him because he tried to take matters into his own hands in fear of losing her.

Look where it got me? Rylan now knew before he could go any further, it was imperative that he get his feelings under control. Keeping silent in seeing her leave was hard for him, much harder than he cared to admit.

"But ye, brethren, are not in darkness, that that day should overtake you as a thief.

Ye are all the children of light, and the children of the day: we are not of the night, nor of darkness."

1 Thessalonians 5:4-5

CHAPTER SIX

"They're home! They're home! Mama, come quick." Katherine shouted from her place on the porch when she saw a carriage come over the green hill. She didn't care to wait for everyone to come outside before she got to her feet to run out and meet them.

As soon as Scarlette and Brenna saw Katherine, they laughed and waved at her. Katherine jumped up and down until the carriage came to a halt and they emerged. She then dropped the doll she held and ran to Scarlette first, letting out a satisfied sigh when she was met by her older sister's warm embrace. By the time it was Brenna turn, the rest of the family eagerly approached.

"We're so glad your home!" Lanna greeted and waited until the children received their hugs. Everyone was talking as fast as they could in a whirlwind of excitement about everything that had gone on during the summer.

"We're so glad to be home," Scarlette and Brenna exclaimed while they were bombarded with excited siblings.

Stephen, who had gone to fetch them, finished directing the servants with the luggage, then went to his wife's side for a brief kiss and to take Audrey from her.

"Oh, I missed you pure much!" Lanna finally wrapped her arms around Scarlette, "We all have," then to Brenna. Tears were present in all three women by the time Lanna slowly released Brenna. Yet, before stepping away, Lanna gazed at Brenna more intently. "My, you look…changed, and a wonderful change so'tiz, my dear. It's loike a weight 'as been lifted from ya."

You have no idea! Brenna thought. She didn't know how much of the dramatic details she would eventually reveal, but presently she couldn't speak much for her emotions overwhelmed her. It surprised Brenna how much she'd truly missed this family, her family. The love that came from Stephen, Lanna, and the rest was almost baffling. They treated her no different than their own children. Being away from them for the summer only made it all the more apparent.

"Mother, this is Miss Eleta Tremblay and Miss Pensee Voclain, our ladies maids all the way from France."

"Welcome," Lanna said as they curtsied, "I 'ope you will feel at home here with al' of us. You must be famished. The cook 'as made an early supper. Let's go an' have a leisurely meal so we can 'ear all aboyt the past few months. And you must tell aboyt the difference in ya," Lanna said the last part only to Brenna in a whisper then winked at her.

"It's good to be home," Brenna truly meant it. The place she had wanted to escape from, now felt more like home than ever.

August 1844

With getting everything ready to return home, all the work that waited them once they arrived at Saerlaith, and slowly getting back into the day to day schedule, Rylan had little time for anything else such as seeking God for much needed direction. However, none of that kept him from thinking about Brenna. Not a day went by that he didn't think about her. He would begin to pray during his devotional time, but the moment he would start to ask the Lord what he should do concerning Miss Kinsey, it wasn't long before his focus was interrupted by thoughts of her. He knew he shouldn't be so consumed with someone other than his Heavenly Father yet he found it difficult to focus on anything but her. Rylan was hopelessly captivated.

He became frustrated with himself once again and finally decided to get out of his study for a while.

"My work can wait," Rylan muttered to himself and quickly got up from his desk where he'd been catching up on things. He was on a mission.

No staff dared to stop him or even speak to Rylan as he marched outside and through the gardens. He was on an assignment to get his thoughts under control and to inquire of the Lord once and for all. He wanted to get as far away from anyone so not to be disturbed. He walked along the edge of two entire fields before he reached a completely secluded spot.

"Lord, I need You." Rylan had just arrived at the chosen place when he raised his hands and spoke aloud as if God stood there with him. "I need Your help. I need to know what You would have me do. I don't want to lean on my own understanding. Please direct my path as Your Word says. You said that if we ask for wisdom, You will give it freely," Rylan looked up at the clear blue sky. He then closed his eyes to wait. It was only a matter of minutes before thoughts of Brenna invaded. "No…I can't think about her right now!" He gazed back up at the sky, "Not until I receive Your guidance." Nothing. "I will not leave here until You show me what to do!" Rylan shouted, yet he knew God wouldn't hear him any better. He continued to pace and pray. Nearly an hour had gone by and he was now lying on the high green grass. He still hadn't gotten an answer.

Maybe I shouldn't have said I would remain here until I receive an answer. This may take a while. The thought had just come to him when it happened! Something rose up in Rylan from deep inside of him.

"You're not listening for anything other than what you want to hear." It struck him like a punch in the stomach.

"What? I haven't heard anything whatsoever. Of course I'll agree to anything You tell me to do," he swiftly spoke, though deep down Rylan knew it might not be true. There was no use in hiding anything from the Lord. "Alright, You are right…of course You're right," Rylan got to his knees, lifted his head, and sighed. "I don't want to lose her. But I know You…my God! I know doing Your will is the only way for me. It's what I choose. It's the only thing that will bring true happiness and satisfaction and bring You glory. I purpose to do whatever it is You tell me. Please help me. What is the first step? Does this mean I must forget her completely?"

"You can't pursue her further until you can surrender your will to mine." His answer wasn't exactly what Rylan had hoped for. It was vague, something he wasn't inclined to.

How long will it take to surrender? When do I know I'm ready? Although Rylan was happy for some direction, it still held too many questions. Should he ask for more instruction? *Well…I guess this would be faith...to just do what He tells me.* "I trust You completely! I surrender Brenna, my love for her, and my will to You. I give You my desires. I know whatever You ask of me, You will enable me to carry out. Thank You for the strength I'll need. In Jesus' Name, amen." While he had surrendered his heart, his mind was another matter. His mind seemed to wait until the moment he'd said amen to immediately blast him with doubts.

It will be too late. Brenna will certainly find someone else. You saw all the gentlemen callers interested in her. It only takes one for you to be out for good. Rylan stood as thoughts of Miss Kinsey seemed to surround him. It was an internal fight, but Rylan was not about to lose. He might not quite know how to go about surrendering or what the next step looked like, but he would keep his eyes on Jesus through it. Trust was the only sure step in front of him and he meant to take it

CHAPTER SEVEN

September 1844

hildren, I'm sorry to interrupt, but it's time for bed."

"Oh mother…Brenna was just telling us another story of the Season!" Lanna glanced at Brenna to see if Katherine was correct.

"I'm nearly finished. It won't take long." Brenna smiled in return.

"Alright, then it's off to bed with ya."

"Yay!" Katherine and Tully shouted for joy. It did nothing to wake little Audrey who'd fallen asleep on the couch.

Lanna sat down next to Stephen as Brenna continued.

"Nothing the poor lady did would stop her horse from coughing. The couple made quite a scene while she began to shout and screech, 'Make it stop! Make it stop!'" Brenna mimicked the woman. "It wasn't until she swatted at her husband that he dismounted his own horse and forced her steed to walk a bit, before it finally seized." Lanna and Stephen couldn't help but join in their children's laughter. "The end," Brenna pronounced, followed by sad groans in protest. Tully, Katherine, the twins, and Stephen Jr. obediently stood to give their parents a kiss before scooting off to bed.

"Don't get up, Mother. I'll help Tully and put Audrey to bed," Scarlette offered.

"Why thank you. Goodnight, dear."

"Goodnight."

Brenna gazed at the fire and didn't notice she was now alone with Lanna and Stephen.

"Brenna, we never got a chance to speak of somethin'."

"Oh yes! I'd forgotten." Brenna turned to them. Lanna faced Stephen to inform him of what they spoke of, though the entire household had witnessed the pleasant change that had taken place in the young lady since her return.

"I'd like to find out as well," Stephen replied when his wife had told him.

"T'be sure, you don't have to. We're just so excited for you. I completely understan' if you wud rather not," Lanna mentioned. There was a time when Brenna hardly spoke to them, much less share something as dear as this. But all was different now. She might not tell everything of her darkest times, knowing their love for her made her not want anything between them.

"I do want to," Brenna said, "When I arrived in London, I had more troubling dreams. I couldn't find relief from anything...until I came across a Bible."

Thank the Lord! Lanna rejoiced within herself. She'd gone to Brenna countless times since adopting her, trying to get her to read from The Bible. She told her it would help, but before, Brenna wanted absolutely nothing to do with it. Both Lanna and Stephen tried to hide their tears of joy as Brenna went on.

"I read almost all the time, as much as I could between outings and parties. It helped so much. It brought me peace...so much peace." Lanna couldn't keep her tears at bay any longer. It's what they'd been praying for so long. "It took a while, but eventually I had no more dreams. I haven't had one since the Season ended...not a fearful or troubling one anyway. And...that's it," Brenna shrugged and did her best to keep her voice from cracking.

"We are so happy for ya!" Lanna got up and embraced her. "I'm glad you've foun' peace. Not only a peace, but the Lord's own peace, with everlastin' contentment and joy. The Word is the only place you can find it."

"I wouldn't have found the truth without you," Brenna gently pulled away to find Stephen at their side. She took his hand.

"And you also."

"Thank God," Stephen grinned.

"Bonjour Miss," Pensee entered Brenna's room after knocking.

"Good morning. How are you?" Brenna asked and put her Bible away to ready for the day.

"Veree well. Did you sleep well?"

"Yes." It felt good to be able to say it truthfully. She couldn't remember ever having such pleasant, peaceful rests since her mother had passed.

"I brought ziss letter for you," Pensee handed her an envelope.

"More interesting mail I suppose. The callers from the Season don't give up easily."

"It makes for interesting reading zough," Pensee chuckled.

"That is true." Ever since leaving London, Scarlette and Brenna received mail, more like love letters, almost daily. They were from perfect strangers, confessing their love and affection. Sometimes, Brenna didn't know if it was meant for her or not by the oddity of some letters.

Brenna opened the letter and began to read it silently. Pensee watched her face grow serious.

Miss Brenna Kinsey
Dolbury, England

August 15, 1844
London, Engand

Dearest Miss Kinsey,

I've thought long and hard about our last meeting and I realized I was utterly wrong about everything. I would like to apologize for everything I said about your family and the entire situation. I also want to extend my deepest regret that I didn't come to you sooner to tell you face to face. Please forgive me. I hope to see you again sometime, although I don't know when. My parents and I leave London in the morning to make the journey home to Saerlaith in Ireland. I indeed hope and pray all works out for you in the future.

Respectfully yours,

Rylan

Brenna finished reading, set the letter on her lap, and gazed ahead. Because she seemed to be deep in thought, Pensee said nothing as she went to the closet to pick out a dress. Brenna wasn't stunned but a bit surprised by finally hearing from him. Except for Hephzibah, no one had ever asked for her forgiveness before.

He wasn't even to blame. I dreadfully overreacted, she thought and felt lonely all of a sudden. A loneliness mixed with longing. Her feelings for Lord Quenell that had subsided with being away from the charming man for a time, now all came back to her. *Lord, what should I do? What can I do?* It was only then she remembered she wasn't alone in her room. She turned to Pensee, who quickly glanced at her in return. Her ladies maid didn't want to be nosey, yet Brenna looked at her as if she wanted to ask her something.

"I hope everysinc is alright," she nonchalantly said as she lay out Brenna's clothing. Pensee looked back to her and found Brenna extending the letter to her! It was the last thing Pensee thought would happen. Some time ago, after forcing Pensee into secrecy when they'd come back from The London Port in the east side, Brenna decided it safe to explain to her ladies maid a little further. Because Brenna knew it remained safe with her, she felt confident to tell her more in hopes of gaining another approach and suggestions.

Brenna patted the bed for Pensee to sit before she began reading. She soon finished and pursed her lips in thought.

"What do you think about it?"

"It is veree nice. It's not often zat a man realizes he is in zee wrong and even apologizes." There wasn't much else she could say since she hadn't heard the quarrel or what it was about.

"What do you think I should do? I mean, honestly…he wasn't in the wrong. I overreacted and let my temper get away from me," Brenna confessed.

"By zee looks of ziss letter, he obviously wants you to know where he is located, no? And zee way he signed with only his first name, not even his title of peerage makes me sink he wants to reveal zat he cares for you." Now Brenna was very glad she allowed Pensee to have a look. Otherwise, she would have never noticed those things.

"Well, perhaps I'll think on it more and pray about it for some time before replying."

"Wise decision…giving it some time can't hurt." Pensee handed Brenna back the letter and Brenna placed it in the top drawer of her writing desk.

"I know I must tell him I'm the one who should be sorry." For the remainder of the day, she kept thinking about it and the way she longed to see him again.

It was nearly two weeks later when Brenna finally wrote back to Rylan. The wait wasn't only to come up with something to say, but Brenna didn't want to appear too desperate with a swift reply. She couldn't help but wonder if they would ever see each other again, but at least they both made attempts to make things right, instead of the quarrel being their last memory.

CHAPTER EIGHT

October 1844

The Right Honourable
Rylan Lennox, Earl of Quenell
Galway, Ireland

September 21, 1844
Dolbury, England

Dear Lord Quenell,

I was glad to receive your letter. I hope all is well with you and your family in Ireland. Only one thing in your letter proved to be untrue. You were not to blame, for it was I who overreacted. What you said was right. Anyone is bound to say the same thing about my situation upon first hearing of it. Of course I forgive you, although it is not necessary. Thank you for your kindness during the Season and thank you for helping me that day. I don't know what I would have done without you.

Warmest regards,

Brenna

December 1844

The Right Honourable
Rylan Lennox,
Earl of Quenell
Talway, Ireland

September 20, 1844
Gresham Detective Agency
Boston, Massachusetts

Lord Quenell,

Upon receiving your letter, I immediately began my search for the name you mentioned. Unfortunately, I didn't get very far. Some people I questioned said Mr. William Dorcet once owned a bank here in Boston, yet ever since he sold it, it has gone to a few different owners. When I went to the church it was told to me they might have attended, I found they recently had a fire so any and all papers concerning births, deaths, or baptisms, were destroyed. People recognize the last name of Dorcet, but don't know where they've gone. It seems this family either disappeared or didn't exist in the first place. I can extend my search to the surrounding towns if you so desire. With your word, I will continue my endeavors.

Sincerely,

Mr. Waite Gresham, Private Investigator

"Thank you, Stuart. That will be all," Rylan glanced up at the footman, who waited in case he wished to reply.

"Yes, My Lord." With that, Stuart left. Rylan rubbed his hands together before putting his gloves back on.

He found nothing. It was a good thing I didn't tell Brenna of writing to Boston in the first place.

Because he had purposed to let her go months earlier, Rylan realized for the first time that he hardly thought of her anymore. The spell Brenna unintentionally held over him seemed to be broken. Even in receiving her letter nearly two months earlier, it hadn't invaded his every thought like it would have previously.

There was no reason to pursue the Dorcet mystery any further, although, there was something that kept him from dropping the situation entirely. Was there more going on than he knew of?

Lord, what does this letter mean? I've given her to You, but...are You trying to show me something else as well? Rylan folded the letter and placed it in his pocket. He decided to go for another ride before going inside. He didn't know where, but he needed to think and pray. Thankfully, it wasn't overly cool despite the dusting of snow on the ground.

Rylan had ridden up the coast for an hour, still without any certain direction. Before he knew it, Rylan, atop his steed, wandered into a small village. It was no more than a mere street of rundown buildings in very ill repair. The owners made the best use of what they had to try and make a living, no matter how sad it was. As he approached, a man emerged from one of the shops and was locking up, most likely for lunch. When the man turned from the door, whistling a cheerful tune, Rylan recognized him.

"If it isn't Colm Brodie...closing for lunch, are you?"

"Lord Quenell! What do I owe the pleasure of seein' you al' the way over 'ere?" Colm neared Rylan's horse, "I was aboyt ter have a bite." Colm could tell almost immediately that something was bothering him. Ever since he had returned to his homeland and gotten married, they'd been tenants to Rylan's family, Rylan only being a youth at the time. Because of his landlord's rare kindness that was unusual in Ireland, Colm frequently interacted with Rylan and his family. The Lennox's didn't treat the Irish like trash and slaves as many other English did. Colm had seen Rylan grow equally as kind as his father. Their frequent talks here and there made it easy for Colm to detect something amiss his usual easy going and cheerful self.

"You know…me wife actually packed me lunch and since it's such a nice day for the beginnin' of December…want ter join me outside?"

"If it's not too much bother, I believe I'll take you up on it." Rylan dismounted his horse, took the reins in hand, and followed Colm to a spot by the stony cliffs, where they sat on some fairly warm rocks overlooking the ocean.

Rylan genuinely enjoyed his talks with Colm because their conversation was almost always surrounded by the faith they shared. At first, they spoke of normal everyday things such as the weather, the crop, and what was new with each of them. A moment finally presented itself when Colm could ask what he'd noticed at the start.

"Is there somethin' botherin' ya?"

"Is it that obvious?" Rylan sighed heavily, confirming his assumptions.

"Well, I've known you for a long time, lad. It makes it al' the more apparent to see there's somethin' weighin' 'eavily on ya." Rylan wanted to tell him everything. He trusted him and his advice, but did asking mean Rylan was picking the matter up again, instead of leaving it in God's hands? However, when he asked himself this very question, the response was different than he expected. It wasn't simply to leave it in His hands. It was as if he was to look into something further.

What is there to look into? Nothing! All dead ends. Well, if he was to indeed dig deeper into the unknown, it surely wouldn't hurt to speak of it, especially with a fellow believer.

"While I was in London, I met someone."

"Oh?" Colm began to smile while Rylan quickly went on.

"It was someone I knew I'd come across before. It wasn't until much later that I learned it was the same young lady I'd helped years earlier. It's a long tale, but by the end of the Season,

54

I grew to admire her…very much."

"So what part is troublin' ya?"

"The way we parted ways…I said some things I regret immensely. We quarreled and she ended up leaving before I could get a chance to apologize. I wrote to her explaining things and she's written back to say she's forgiven me."

"I still don't see anythin' troublin' aboyt it. No harm done, I'd say," Colm stated.

"Since returning to Ireland, I couldn't stop thinking about her. I finally went to God about it and He told me I had to give her to Him before He could lead me."

"And did you heed Him?"

"I did as He said…yet now…." Rylan placed his hand over his pocket where the letter from the investigator was, "After all this time, I succeeded in at least not having Brenna Kinsey consume my every thought." Colm had just taken a bite of his bread when he began to choke. Rylan didn't hear as he finished.

"It seems different than before," Rylan glanced at Colm when he realized he wasn't merely clearing his throat, but choking! "Are you alright?"

"I…think…so," Colm hit his fist against his chest a few times from inhaling his food, "What did you say her name was?" he finally asked when he could speak again.

"Brenna Kinsey."

"Oh," Colm sighed, "I must have 'eard wrong before…I thought—"

"As a matter of fact," Rylan unintentionally interrupted him because he'd just remembered, "She told me she was adopted. If I remember right, her previous surname was Dorcet."

"Wait…what?" Colm's breath caught in his throat and he nearly choked all over again.

"Dorcet, Brenna Dorcet." Rylan repeated and glanced at Colm in question. *What is he so confused about?*

"That is impossible!"

"How so?" Now Rylan was completely confused.

"It's impossible because I nu a Brenna Dorcet. An' she…well, I don't nu how she could be in Englan'. She and her family live in Boston…America."

"How do you know her? Are you certain you aren't thinking of someone else?"

"I'm for certain cos Brenna is me sister's daughter. My niece!" Colm rubbed his face in astonishment.

"How can it be? She is in England though. This is just…I don't know how this can be!" The moment Rylan said it, he knew it was foolishness. He knew fully well that all things were possible with God and nothing was mere chance with Him. He had a plan. It was God's plan for him to run into Colm Brodie and to find all of this out from him. So instead of asking how it could be and how impossible it was, Rylan instantly made a choice to get past all of that and simply go with it. He would listen to Colm and be led for his next step.

"When I spoke to Brenna the last time, she told me she was locked in a trunk and the next thing she knew, she was bound for England. This was several years ago. If it was an accident or on purpose, she didn't say."

"This is truly no coincidence," Colm voiced Rylan's exact thoughts. "Has Brenna been in contact with 'er family? Do they nu where she is? Did I 'ear ya say she was adopted or somethin'?"

"Yes she was. There are more unfortunate things that have happened to her, and it was some time before she was able to write to her family, sadly without any response."

"That's odd."

"I thought the same. But it's all true then? Her family is from Boston?" Rylan asked just to be sure.

"Aye."

"Well, why won't they respond?"

"I don't nu. They must be pure worried and searchin'. I can't think av any reason. Whaen I returned ter Ireland to take over me uncle's shop, Brenna's parents had only just married. Brenna wasn't born yet. I used to receive letters fairly often. The last letter from Kylene, my sister and Brenna's mum, mentioned she was in the family way, Brenna bein' aboyt age ten at the time. That wus the last I 'eard from her. A year went by before we got word that she'd passed away in childbirth."

"Nothing after that?" Rylan asked as Colm shook his head solemnly. "After we parted ways, I wrote to an investigator in America to look into it further and I received a reply just today." Rylan pulled it from his pocket to show Colm, "He didn't find anything."

"Really? William inherited a large bank."

"The investigator found nothing of the like. There are no banks owned by him, at least, not anymore. I should write to Brenna again to tell her about finding all this out and finding you!" All of a sudden, something dawned on Rylan. It was something Colm had said.

"Wait, so your sister is Brenna's mother…Brenna is Irish?"

"Aye?"

"Funny, she never mentioned it." All at once, something quickened inside of him like a sort of go ahead, urging him forward. *She knows I'm Irish and of my family's past, yet it made no difference to her,* Rylan thought. Ever since he could remember, it's all that seemed to matter. All his life he'd been surrounded by separation between the Irish and English. Other than his family, society never stopped showing him in various ways that he was inferior.

But Brenna is different. Besides her faith, was this another difference he had seen in her from the very start? *Lord, what does all of this mean?* Because the urge to act became increasingly stronger, Rylan stood to his feet. He now knew what he must do and do quickly.

"What is it?" Colm glanced up from the letter to Rylan only to see him going for his horse, "Where are ye headin'?"

"There's no time to explain," Rylan climbed atop his steed,

"I'll send word as soon as I can." With that, he rode away with considerable speed.

He went directly home. As soon as he entered the front door, he called to the nearby staff.

"Molly, could you pack some things for me as quickly as possible?"

"Certainly, My Lord. How long should I plan for?"

"About a month."

"Yes, My Lord." Molly immediately dropped what she was doing to heed his orders. Rylan then turned to a footman.

"Please ready my carriage. I must leave at once."

"Yes, My Lord." Lastly, he glanced at the butler, who'd just approached.

"May I be of assistance?"

"Could you inform my parents that I had to leave for some time and that I'm sorry it was so sudden. Oh, and please ask Mr. McConahay to oversee things while I'm gone. I'm not sure how long I'll be away."

"Yes, My Lord. Not to worry," Hughes replied.

"Thank you." Rylan was surprised to see the maid already return with his bag in hand. He was able to leave in a matter of minutes.

"Excuse me, where are you headed?" Rylan shouted from his place in the carriage once they reached the harbor. He knew one of the three ships docked there had to be going to England. Fog was coming off of the water and it mingled with the visible breaths coming from the men working on the shore. It was even more so since most of them were hard at work.

"Bound to Scotland," a nearby sailor, busy loading one of the ships shouted back, then went on with his business.

"Please drive on to the next ship," Rylan instructed his driver. "Please Lord, let one be headed to England," he whispered. Otherwise, he would have to wait at least another week before the opportunity would arise again.

"You there! Where are you bound to?" He had to shout again even louder to get one of the men's attention.

"England, Sir."

"Splended. Could I gain passage on your vessel?"

"Aye, we're full up and leaving any time now," the sailor began to turn away but Rylan wasn't about to give up easily. He quickly got out of his carriage, grabbed his bag, and followed the man, who'd picked up a crate and was headed to the gangplank.

"I'm willing to pay a fair price straight away and I'm ready to leave now. All I need is a place to sit out of the way."

"You'd best speak to the captain," the sailor grunted, "There he is now," he then nodded his head in the captain's direction, "Captain, this bloke would like passage." Before the man could reply, Rylan spoke up for himself.

"I'm willing to pay anything you like."

"Alright. You'll have to find any room you can. Might be a place among the crew. No fancy cabins for your liking."

"That's fine."

"We sail about now so come aboard." Rylan gave a quick wave to his driver to let him know he could return to Saerlaith without him.

"Thank You, Lord," he breathed his thanks.

It was some time before Rylan found a suitable place for himself among the sailor's sleeping quarters deep inside the lower deck. It was quite crowded from each man's few belongings, hammocks, various crates, and trunks, but at least it was warm. Rylan laid out his meager belongings for the journey and was glad to find himself alone for the time being. Since being strongly urged onward only hours earlier, Rylan hadn't gotten a chance to gather his thoughts, much less converse with his

Father. He dearly hoped he hadn't misunderstood His leading now that he was well on his way to England.

"Lord, am I doing the right thing?"

CHAPTER NINE

December 1844

renna looked up and watched the large clouds move steadily across the cheerful blue sky. She slowly walked down the street, feeling carefree. The gentle breeze at her back tugged at her free flowing hair as if showing her the way. She began to think the way the few leaves floated by her, that it almost seemed unreal. However, it did little to sway her as she continued on with her walk.

What a perfect day! I wonder if— Brenna's thoughts came to a startling halt when she approached another street that met the one she was walking on. She stood still, though the wind kept pulling at her skirts, beckoning her to keep going. When she gazed down the way, she realized it wasn't another street at all, but an alley way. There was fog coming from deep inside it, bringing with it no fear or dread. Instead, it held only mystery, so much so, that Brenna began to step towards it. It wasn't until she finally stood in the same place as her many dreams that she recalled the familiar place. She marveled that it took her all this time to figure it out. It wasn't at all like the countless times before. This time it was daylight and the alley was cleaner and brighter as the sun shined into it. When the bright light met the fog, it made it become whiter than any lamp or candle, almost heavenly. It was like a large cloud, descending around her.

Brenna could hardly believe this place that had once brought her so much anxiety and horror, now held comfort. She heard no frightening noise from behind like someone following her while she walked in further. When she reached the spot where Hephzibah had once lain, there was nothing there, not one piece of rubbish. Brenna almost had to shield her eyes from the brightness as she looked ahead and saw the strong hand come out to her. Peace and safety came from it. She couldn't help but hesitate for a moment, waiting for this wonderful place to end in horror like the previous times. Yet, nothing happened. Nothing lurked behind. All was completely calm as the hand still reached out to her. Would she reach it this time and see who it belonged to at long last? With each hopeful and exhilarating thought, Brenna took another step. She felt so light and peaceful as if she was floating. She was entirely enveloped in the bright cloud, her gaze fixed on the hand.

Brenna couldn't believe it when the hand was before her and still the dream continued on. With a satisfied sigh of relief, she placed her hand in the warm hand, much larger than her own. She had never felt more safe or secure as the hand gently squeezed hers as if telling her all would be alright. Suddenly the figure, whom the hand belonged to, took a step toward her out of the fog and shadows. When Brenna very slowly glanced up to see his face her breath caught within her. There, out of the mist, was Rylan. He gazed at her with a look of affection, assuring her that he would never leave her. He drew her closer and was about to speak when a loud crash made her jump in surprise.

"Sacre bleu! I'm so sorree, Miss…very sorree for my clumziness!" Brenna quickly sat up in bed to find Pensee kneeling on the floor. She must have been carrying a wash basin with fresh water, only to drop it. There was water and shattered pieces of porcelain all over the floor.

"I didn't mean to wake you. It slipped right out of my 'and. Voila…I'm a clumsy oaf."

"It's alright," Brenna reassured once she had awaken enough to realize her whereabouts and what had happened. "It was only an accident," she continued when she noticed Pensee was nearly in tears as she began to gather the broken pieces of glass. "Are you alright?"

"Oui," Pensee had it cleaned up in no time and wouldn't let Brenna help her at all.

Once the ladies maid left, Brenna sat back against her pillow and sighed as she gently rubbed her eyes.

What a wonderful dream that was. Although no one was to blame, Brenna was a little frustrated to have the most wonderful dream she'd ever had, interrupted. *And right before he was about to speak! What was he going to say?* Because it was still so real to her, Brenna had to remind herself that anything between them, or anything she thought or even hoped was between them was over. Rylan was in Ireland, back to his own life. They might have written to apologize for the way their last meeting had ended, but their quarrel before parting ways seemed to put a damper on all the other times they had shared together. The dream made her regret it all the more. It was over and she knew she must accept it and move on. However, after the romantic dream, Brenna knew it would be difficult to do so. She sat and pondered over it for some time before getting her Bible out to read.

"The night is far spent, the day is at hand: let us therefore cast off the works of darkness, and let us put on the armour of light."

Romans 13:12

CHAPTER TEN

January 1845

The carriage lurched to a slow stop. Rylan looked out to see a spacious house surrounded by thin trees and a slight dusting of snow. The sight was a warm welcome with the glow of lights coming from the windows and smoke rising from the chimneys. It finally occurred to him what time of the day it was. The sun had just set and the sky was quickly darkening. With everything going on at the busy harbor, the commotion upon the ship's arrival, searching for directions and someone to take him, Rylan completely lost track of time.

I hope it's not too late to call, he thought. Since he'd come all this way, Rylan hated the thought of waiting any longer.

"This is Caragin," the driver informed.

"And the Kinsey's live here?" Rylan wanted to be certain. When the driver nodded, Rylan replied, though a bit embarrassed. "I just need a moment," he leaned back as his nervousness returned. During the journey, Rylan grew rather nervous with the thought of what he was about to do. However, he quickly reassured himself that he was indeed doing the right thing. It was the only thing that helped to calm his racing heart.

Rylan took a deep breath, searched his heart one last time, then stood to his feet. He climbed out of the carriage and walked to the house with purpose.

The knock at the door made everyone stop what they were doing to glance at the doorway leading to the front entrance. The children looked at their parents in question.

"Who cud it be at this time?" Lanna glanced at Stephen just as they heard the maid go to the door.

"May I help you, sir?"

"I need to see Miss Brenna Kinsey. Does she reside here?"

"Yes, please come in." The minute she allowed him to enter, Rylan began looking for Brenna as if she would be right there. Of course, she wasn't, but he knew he must talk to her as soon as he could before he lost his nerve.

"Please wait here," the maid left him in the entryway. Rylan could barely keep still while he waited. He watched the maid closely as she went to inform the family of their visitor. He shifted from side to side until he couldn't wait any longer. He had to see Brenna!

"There's someone to see you, Miss," Right when the maid entered the drawing room, someone came up behind her in a hurry. Stephen instinctively stood to see what was going on as Rylan scooted past the maid, who flinched in surprise.

"Excuse me…pardon me," he finally saw the one he'd been searching for. Brenna sat among her family. He thought her more beautiful than ever.

When Brenna saw who it was, her eyes widened in shock. Rylan ignored every surprised stare and looked directly at Brenna as he swiftly covered the distance between them.

Can this truly be happening? Is this another dream? she thought. When he approached, he reached out his hand to her exactly like in her dream. Brenna was breathless as she timidly took it and stood very slowly. It was only then that the realization of what he was about to do hit him all at once. All the things Rylan planned to say vanished and in its place was pure emotion, something he wasn't used to. He tried to find the words from his planned speech but couldn't. Brenna gazed up at him expectantly and hopeful. Seeing her again confirmed everything.

"Marry me?" the simple request in a slightly shaky tone, was all he could come up with.

Tears came to Brenna's eyes, her mind telling her over and over, *This is real! This is real!* She had to repeatedly remind herself, for everything around her seemed to tell her otherwise. It felt as if she was in some kind of fog. She was lightheaded, floating, and wonderful all at the same time. Brenna promptly knew what her answer would be. She also knew if she allowed herself to reason and analyze the matter, she wouldn't be able to do it. Instead of listening to her mind, Brenna quickly decided to follow her heart.

"Yes," she would never forget the look of sheer joy that

filled Rylan's eyes, along with a few tears of his own. It took the place of his uncertainty that had risen while he'd waited for her reply.

Since entering their home, Rylan noticed for the first time they weren't alone when he heard a child giggle in the background. He removed his gaze from Brenna and glanced around the room. There, he found several children of various ages sitting on the couch and floor staring up at him. One of which was Katherine. She was obviously the giggling one, for she was leaning against Scarlette and covering her mouth. She was grinning from ear to ear. Next he saw Brenna's mother, who appeared to be quite stunned, and lastly the father of the house. Rylan also noticed that he and Brenna still held hands when Stephen cleared his throat loudly, so he quickly released her.

Brenna too had forgotten the entire family was present. She exchanged glances with Scarlette. She was smiling and looked somewhat surprised but more excited than anything.

"I...I'm sorry to intrude on all of you in this manner," Rylan regained his usual distinguished stature. His valor became all the more obvious to everyone the minute he spoke. No one else really knew what to say.

"Everyone, this is Lord Rylan Lennox, Earl of Quenell." Stephen took on his fatherly role more seriously than ever before. His family, especially the younger ones, watched in wonder as he stepped up to the young man and shook hands.

"Lord Quenell," he formally greeted.

"Please, you can call me Rylan." This was the first of many times he would impress Mr. and Mrs. Kinsey. There were far too few members of peerage that would ever allow anyone to call them by their first name, much less to people below their rank.

"This is my father, Stephen. My mother, Lanna, Scarlette, who you already know, Stephen Jr., the twins Andrew and Philip, Katherine, Tully, and Audrey," Brenna finished the introductions. The second gesture that impressed them all was when Rylan went around the room and made a point to shake everyone's hand, even little Audrey's, with just as much respect and effort as if he'd just met a duke or duchess.

Brenna knew Lanna, along with everyone else, was wondering why she'd never mentioned Lord Quenell from the Season and now he was here proposing! The very thought boggled her own mind. Thankfully, no one voiced their thoughts in front of Rylan.

"Since we've just had the pleasure of meeting you, someone who clearly means a great deal to Brenna, I would like to invite you to stay here at Caragin for a time so that we may get to know you better." Brenna breathed a sigh of relief for how kindly Stephen had put it. She could only imagine what William, her true father, would have done if a perfect stranger had burst in and proposed.

He would most likely chase my suitor out with a weapon! she thought.

"It would be my honor to stay, if it's not imposing on you in any way." In truth, that was another thing Rylan hadn't thought of during his hurried journey. If not for Mr. Kinsey's generous offer, he had no idea what he would have done nor where to stay for the night.

He didn't say anything about it that evening, but Stephen undoubtingly planned to speak to this surprise suitor about his desire to marry Brenna before anything was final in his eyes. And by the look he'd shared with Lanna, she fully agreed with him.

Hours later, Brenna floated up the stairs to at least try to get a little sleep.

Rylan...Earl of Quenell, wants to marry me! Me! Practically an orphan...a nobody in the mind of high society. She replayed the delightful evening in her mind, though the realization of it hadn't had a chance to sink in yet. Brenna rounded the corner of the hall towards her bedroom when she met the grinning Scarlette. Her eyes still danced with excitement.

"Hello," Brenna couldn't help but smile giddily as well.

"Can you believe it? Brenna, you were just proposed to by an earl!" Scarlette grasped Brenna's hands and whispered, although she was quickly growing louder by the end, "And you said yes right away!" she informed as if Brenna needed to be reminded.

"I can hardly grasp it."

"Did you know of his coming at all?"

"No...nothing,"

"Oh my goodness!" Scarlette gasped, "I'm glad he is able to stay. Oh Brenna!" Scarlette hugged her, and then something crossed her mind. "You do know Father will have a talk with him, right?" Brenna's smile momentarily faded.

"What? What kind of talk?"

"Well, I know him and before anything is final, Father must make sure Lord Quenell is...suitable. You know...suitable to marry you, especially when he hardly knows Rylan. I'm sure it will be just fine," Scarlette reassured when Brenna began to appear worried. "You know of his character more than we do. If it's acceptable to you, with a bit more time, Father will see it also. Most importantly, he'll want to find out Rylan's faith and beliefs and such. To be certain you are equally yoked as The Bible calls it." Brenna did recall hearing Lanna and Stephen say something along those lines since returning home from the Season, when Scarlette began to receive letters from one particular gentleman.

"Alright...when do you think this will take place?"

"Most likely as soon as possible. But don't worry over it."

"I won't."

CHAPTER ELEVEN

renna entered the dining room aflutter with excitement and a bit nervous as well. Stephen was seated at the far end of the table with Rylan at his right. In seeing him sitting there and as he looked at her and smiled, it confirmed to Brenna that the wonderful night before wasn't a dream, but very real. She met his smile and tried not to blush as she made her way to the chair across from Rylan.

"Good morning," Rylan spoke and stood along with Stephen until she took a seat.

"Good morning. Did you sleep well?" Brenna glanced at Stephen and found him closely watching their exchange. She quickly recalled Scarlette's words and wondered if Stephen had talked with Rylan yet.

"Very good, and you?" Rylan asked.

"Yes." Neither one of them had slept much, though they didn't consider it a complete loss for they had plenty of lovely things to think on.

After the men sat down again, the rest of the family entered. Katherine and Tully must have forgotten about the visitor, for when they came in they were chattering away until they caught sight of Rylan. They immediately became quiet and stared at him. Lanna brought up the rear, bent over and holding onto Audrey's hands as she slowly waddled in with a proud look on her face.

After saying a prayer, Stephen and Lanna began to casually ask Rylan about himself such as where he was from, what he did, and about his family. Rylan answered each question with ease, without any nervousness as if he'd known them forever. Ever so often, he would look at Brenna and smile warmly. Brenna didn't exactly know what his gaze meant. He seemed to be checking with her from time to time to make sure he was doing alright. This was his time to prove himself. With each swift exchange, he wanted to reassure her that no matter what, he was prepared to do anything it took to win her heart. It only caused Brenna to blush by his affectionate and caring glances.

Everyone else remained silent while Rylan explained what his home was like. Katherine could hold her silence no longer.

"Do you live in a castle?" she asked in anticipation. Lanna was about to tell her it wasn't polite to interrupt and to speak without being addressed, but Rylan spoke first.

"Why no, I don't. Do you?" He spoke to her as an equal and didn't blow her silly question off as she was used to by most visitors. In fact, she was surprised and glad he wasn't stuffy like other grownups.

"This isn't a castle. It's just a house…but sometimes I pretend it is and I'm the princess."

"Well! I didn't know I was in the presence of royalty!" Rylan gave her a playful wink, "Forgive me for not bowing earlier, Princess Katherine." Everyone around the table chuckled, especially Tully and Katherine.

"You're funny!" she nearly squealed. Brenna knew he had instantly won the hearts of her younger siblings.

I hope Stephen will be as easily convinced, she thought.

They talked some time as they finished eating, laughing often before Stephen grew serious.

"Before we go about the rest of the day, might I have a word with you privately?"

"Of course." Both men got to their feet.

"We will only be a moment," Stephen led the way to the library.

Oh…I hope all goes well, Brenna watched them leave. She then met Scarlette's gaze. Since Lanna was busy wiping Tully's face, Scarlette took the opportunity to mouth to Brenna that it would be alright. It did little to lighten her spirits.

"I hope you don't mind that I pulled you away from everyone, but I thought this would be a good time to talk some things over." Stephen shut the door to the library and motioned to Rylan to have a seat in front of the window. He sat in the other chair with a table between them.

"Why certainly," Rylan replied. He knew what Stephen spoke of and rightly so. He was glad to find himself calm and collected in talking with Brenna's father. It was because he was persuaded that he was exactly where the Lord wanted him, at the right timing. Rylan could rest in this fact and was very glad he'd submitted everything to his Heavenly Father that day instead of taking matters into his own hands. As long as he purposed to be led in every step he took, everything would work out.

"I presume you called on my daughter during the Season."

"Yes, at various social occasions."

"What is it about Brenna that is of interest to you over the rest?" Stephen had never done this sort of thing, though he'd long been prepared for it. Ever since Scarlette, his oldest was born, he'd prayed for guidance for the day he'd be approached and asked for his daughter's hand. His specific questions might have been planned out, but they'd changed drastically over the years since marrying Lanna. The things he thought were the most important in life took on a whole new meaning since he'd witnessed his Heavenly Father through his wife's actions. Lanna's entire life was surrounded and consumed with her Savior. As soon as Rylan answered, Stephen would get right down to what truly mattered.

"Since the first time I saw her, I knew she was different. She's not only different from the rest, she is above them. I instantly saw in her actions, towards others also, that she wasn't enthralled with only gaining others attention or trying to make a good match, but something more. To be completely honest with you, Mr. Kinsey, it wasn't until I saw her a few more times that I finally realized what the difference was. It was her faith, and it has made a substantial impression on me. I fully share it and believe a couple can only be truly happy when they share this between them. It's the only way to start a family…on a solid foundation." Stephen was blown away. Rylan took the very words right out of his mouth! He was assuredly convinced then and there.

"I couldn't agree more," Stephen said and was able to remain serious, "Why now? Why have you waited so long after the Season to ask for her hand?" Rylan nearly smiled at the question.

Once again, he was so glad he'd trusted God instead of trying to make it come to pass himself, most likely failing in his attempts.

"After the Season and parting ways, I couldn't stop thinking about Brenna. I asked the Lord to guide my steps, but He showed me before I could be led, I had to render my hopes and purposes to His first. At first it was very difficult. With time I was eventually able to give her to the Lord. I'm glad I did, otherwise I would have tried to make it happen in the wrong timing. After all of that, He gave me the go ahead, you could say." Stephen sat back in his chair and marveled yet again at the young man. All he had revealed spoke volumes of his character.

"Well…I have to say," Stephen began. Rylan couldn't tell what he was thinking by the look of his solemn state and almost guarded tone of voice. Nervousness started to wash over him, but he wouldn't allow it. "I'm quite impressed." Rylan had to bite his tongue to keep from blurting, "Really?"

"Any young man who is inclined to a young woman and chooses to wait on the Lord instead of acting rashly, caring enough to do the right thing instead of following his own feelings, says a lot of you. Furthermore, sharing your heart and faith, not knowing my views on the matter is also very noteworthy and in my opinion, is worthy of my daughter's affection." Rylan wanted to leap for joy! He would have too if no one was watching, much less Brenna's father.

Stephen stood so Rylan did likewise. No one could have wiped the grin from his face.

"I heartily give my blessing," Stephen couldn't keep from smiling any longer in watching the young man's sheer glee and excitement as he extended his hand to him and shook it. "I only ask one thing of you. That you would stay on here at Caragin for at least a fortnight so we might all get to know you better."

"Yes, sir. I would be honored. Thank you."

"What do you say we tell the rest of the family the good news?"

The men left and found the family in the sitting room, all but the boys, who were in another room with a private tutor.

The butterflies in Brenna's stomach that had been slowly settling while she waited, instantly returned at the sight of Rylan and Stephen.

Rylan appears pleased...can I take it as a good sign? she asked herself. Everyone gazed up at Stephen with anticipation.

"I want to inform that I've given my blessing to Rylan and Brenna." The group suddenly erupted with cheers and claps. The completely quiet family in shock the night before had transformed. Lanna and Scarlette jumped to their feet and began congratulating Brenna and Rylan, laughing and talking of plans. The boys came in just then and joined in the well-wishing. Amidst the commotion, Brenna met Rylan's gaze. The brief but meaningful look was one of hope, happiness, and affection. It caused all of Brenna's questions how everything was going to work out, and if she was making the right choice, entirely vanish. There was no doubt in the way he tenderly looked at her, showing how much he loved her. The simple gesture allowed her to see herself marrying him and their future life together in one wonderful moment.

CHAPTER TWELVE

The fresh snow that had fallen during the night now glistened in the morning sunlight. As it sparkled, it seemed to call to the children to come outside to make the first tracks in the perfect, untouched snow. Before their morning lessons started, they bundled up with Rylan and Brenna and embarked. They made snow angels, went sledding, and had a snowball fight before deciding to go for a short walk.

Rylan and Brenna were both glad for a chance to talk when the children ran up ahead of them a little ways, playing and laughing the entire time. At first, they didn't say anything for they didn't know where to start. The past few days had been spent in making plans. They agreed that Rylan would return to Ireland after their quick courtship at Caragin, to ready things there and to bring his parents back for the wedding. Brenna had yet to find out why Rylan had come and proposed when he did. She also wanted to ask what he and Stephen had discussed that day in the library before Stephen had consented. Rylan hadn't brought it up, so she ultimately decided against it for now.

"Tell me about Sirlayeth...what is it like?" Before thinking Rylan chuckled.

"What?" Brenna glanced at him.

"I'm sorry. I didn't mean to laugh. It's just the way you pronounced it, although, it's commonly mistaken...and for good reason. It can be...difficult," he couldn't help but snicker again.

"Well then, Lord Quenell," she said wryly, "Please enlighten me. If I'm to live there, I don't want to be the laughing stock of Ireland." It still sounded so strange to say it and to think she was getting married!

"It is spelled the way you said it. It is pronounced ser-la. It means free ruler. I think you will like it. The view is my favorite. It's right off of the coast and looks out to sea."

"I can't wait to see it...Saerlaith," she repeated the name, "I like it."

They grew quiet again, both pondering over the changes that were about to take place in the near future.

"I have one question," Brenna stopped and turned to face Rylan. "Why did you come back to England? I mean, what made you decide to...." *This was a bad idea! What am I doing?* Brenna scolded herself as her face began to turn red.

"What made up my mind to come and ask you to marry me?" Watching her innocence made Rylan fall in love with her all over again.

"Yes," Brenna looked away and started walking again to try and hide her embarrassment. Rylan quickly caught up and touched the back of her arm to slow.

"God told me to. Well, the truth of it is, I wanted to long ago."

"Really?"

"After the way we parted, I was so ashamed of myself that I couldn't bring myself to. I also wanted to be absolutely certain if I was to pursue you, it would be the Lord's will and timing...to know it wasn't for the wrong reasons. It wasn't until I was able to turn it all over to Him that I could think clearly." Rylan suddenly remembered his talk with Colm Brodie! He'd been so wrapped up in everything and had completely forgotten about the divine connection. "And an amazing thing happened! I came across someone...well," Rylan chuckled at the profound coincidence and irony of it all, "I've actually known him for years. Anyway, before departing for England, I found out he's someone you know."

"Who?"

"Colm Brodie," he asked when Brenna didn't say anything right away. "Do you know him?"

"Wait...he is my—oh, I know that name."

"He told me he's your uncle. Isn't it amazing?"

"Oh that's right! Oh my...I used to hear a lot about him from my mother. He left shortly after my parents married."

"Brenna!" A shout came from up ahead, "I'm cold!" Andrew wiped his red nose and sniffed.

"Alright, let's go back to the house." Although their talk was brief, Brenna was still glad for the short time they had together.

Brenna had just finished dressing for dinner and made her way downstairs to rejoin the rest of the family. Along the way, she heard someone playing the piano in the parlor. At first, she presumed it to be Scarlette, but the closer she got she heard a man singing softly along with it.

Who could it be? Once she went to the room and peaked inside, she was surprised to find Rylan sitting at the piano and singing. He was all alone. *He must be waiting for the rest of us,* Brenna thought by the casual relaxed way he quietly fingered the keys and how softly he sang, not to attract attention to himself. Brenna watched him and thought it was lovely. He was very good. It seemed that Rylan was humble in all he did. Brenna had witnessed far too many high society gentlemen sing loudly with large showy gestures, trying to show everyone how wonderful they were. Not at all like Rylan. She thought his voice, while playing was far superior to any she'd heard during the Season, though she didn't know the song. It took a little while to catch some of the words to realize he sang about God. His sincerity and the way he sang the words showed he and his Heavenly Father were no strangers to one another.

She eventually thought she shouldn't spy on him any longer. She was about to make herself known when she heard a noise coming from the other entrance of the room. Katherine, Tully, and one of the twins must have finished getting dressed before the rest and made their way into the room. They were laughing about something until they were made aware of Rylan's presence. Brenna stayed where she was and watched Rylan's reaction.

"Well, hello there," he swung around on the piano bench to face the children.

"You play the piano really good," Tully exclaimed in his little, sometimes hard to understand, voice.

"Thank you."

"Please play another!" Katherine put in.

"If you like," Rylan lifted Tully onto the seat next to him as the other two came closer. Rylan began to play a silly tune that made them all giggle.

"Mr. Lennox, did you know I'm learning how to play?"

"Is that right? Do you know London Bells?" Katherine shook her head.

"Would you like me to show you?"

"Yes, please!" she squealed with delight.

Brenna smiled when she saw how quickly they had taken to Rylan, and as she kept watching, it appeared that he was equally as taken with them. She tried not to get ahead of herself, but she couldn't help but picture Rylan playing with their future children.

By the time Brenna finally stepped in the room, Rylan had lifted Tully onto his lap and Katherine was sitting beside them, learning the song. Philip watched them play while chuckling from time to time. In a way, Brenna wanted to see what Rylan would do once he saw her. She was happy to see that he glanced at her and grinned, not embarrassed in the least.

"Do you think we should teach her the song as well?" Rylan leaned in as if telling a secret to the children. Their eyes danced with pleasure. "Although, this song might be a bit too difficult for her, don't you think?"

"Hey!" Brenna scolded playfully.

"There ya al' are," Lanna entered, holding Audrey on her hip. "You aren't botherin' our special guest, are ya?"

"No," Tully and Katherine answered in unison.

"Not at all. They both play very well," Rylan reassured.

"Is that so?" Lanna asked enthusiastically as they rushed to her side.

"Mr. Lennox taught me a new song!"

"You will 'av to tell me all about it durin' dinner because it's ready to be served."

"For then shalt thou have thy delight in the Almighty, and shalt lift up thy face unto God.

Thou shalt make thy prayer unto him, and he shall hear thee, and thou shalt pay thy vows.

Thou shalt also decree a thing, and it shall be established unto thee: and the light shall shine upon thy ways."

Job 22:26~28

CHAPTER THIRTEEN

"*I*s this the edge of Caragin then?" Rylan glanced at Stephen Jr. and pointed to the brown colored ridge, spotted with snow, before them.

"No, it goes a bit further. There is a valley over this hill. Our land ends when it begins to rise again," he replied.

"I see. It is beautiful countryside here. The hills make me forget I'm not in Ireland, though, all the trees here give it away." Rylan and Brenna rode side by side with Stephen Jr. acting as chaperone and guide.

After the snowfall only two days ago, things began to warm up a little. The glistening snow was all but gone from the sunshine. It left the ground brown and wet, which made it feel like fall again. But neither Rylan nor Brenna noticed much of it.

"It's actually getting warm out," Brenna unbuttoned her heavy cloak, removed it, and draped it over her horse.

"Do you want to return to the house?" Rylan asked.

"Only if you and Stephen want to. It's probably nearing lunch time."

"If we ride to that hill and around the edge of the valley, it will be a quicker ride," Stephen Jr. suggested.

"Alright," Rylan then glanced at Brenna, "If it's not too steep for you."

"Oh no. In fact, I say we race!"

"What? But you're...riding sidesaddle!"

"I'm quite capable. It's all I've ever known." Brenna's eyes glistened at the challenge. She might have overcome her selfish and spoiled ways, but her competitive spirit was a whole other matter. Brenna clicked to her horse and slowly moved forward at Rylan's hesitation. She looked back at him and flashed him a rueful grin.

"If you're worried I might lose, you can always give me a head start!" She then dug her heels into her steed and shouted, "To the far ridge then!" and was off.

Rylan looked at Stephen Jr., who was laughing as if this was an everyday occurrence.

"Well you heard her..to the far ridge!" Stephen stated and hurried his horse along. Rylan then let himself relax and started after them. He had to admit Brenna's riding was exceptional. He scolded himself for thinking the less of her.

The men were easily gaining speed on the level terrain but it soon became more difficult as they neared the valley. Rylan had to pull back on his reigns a little when he began to descend. His horse didn't seem to realize how steep it was swiftly becoming and wanted to keep going at full speed.

"Whoa…whoa…." He pulled harder and glanced ahead to where Brenna was also slowing down about twenty feet in front of him. The hill was deceptive from the top, looking down. It wasn't until half way down when Rylan saw how steep it truly was.

Does the Kinsey family do this sort of thing often? he wondered. He was about to look back up at Brenna to tell her to be careful, when to his horror, he saw Brenna's horse lose its footing. It stumbled and gave way, causing it to roll and taking Brenna with it!

"Brenna!" Rylan shouted, though he was helpless to do anything other than watch the horse roll on top of her petite body before nearing the bottom of the hill. She now lay deathly still.

"Dear Lord, let her be alright! Let her be alive!" Forlorn prayers flowed from Rylan as he hurried to get to her. As soon as he was near enough, he jumped off his horse and ran to Brenna. She was lying on her back, eyes wide with fear and shock, and breathing heavily. She gasped for air, desperately trying to breathe. Her horse was a few feet from her. Other than its frightened neighing and panting, it was miraculously standing.

Rylan fell to his knees at Brenna's side. He was relieved to see her breathing although, there was a considerable amount of blood on her face coming from her nose. When she was able to look up at him briefly before closing her eyes, he knew something was horribly wrong from the sound of her labored gasps.

Rylan glanced at Stephen Jr., who was almost to them.

"Go get help!" he screamed, "Hurry!" Stephen immediately headed to the right of them as fast as he could. As soon as he was out of sight, Rylan reached for Brenna's cloak that she'd removed earlier, bunched it up, and gently placed it under her head. He then took her hand.

"Lord, I know You wouldn't bring us together…just to have

her leave me. You love her more than I do…I pray that You would touch her body and strengthened her. Cover her in Your blood for she's Your child. You are the Lord of her life. She's in covenant with You and no weapon formed against her shall prosper," Rylan's voice quivered with emotion as Brenna continued to try and catch her breath, "I speak to her body and I command it to be healed and completely made whole now. You will live and not die!" tears filled his eyes, "Do you hear me? You will live and not die, in Jesus name!" He raised her hand to his lips and kissed it.

As they waited for help to come, Brenna's breathing slowly became more normal and even. Rylan silently thanked God when Stephen Jr. returned with his father and mother in a wagon with three servants riding behind. By the time they carefully brought Brenna to the house, the doctor was waiting for them. The entire family, including Rylan rejoiced when the doctor informed them nearly an hour later that Brenna's unnatural breathing was the result of getting the wind knocked out of her. Other than a few scrapes and bruises, it was nothing short of a miracle.

It wasn't long before Brenna was able to leave her room. Other than a little sore, she felt good. After all she had endured, everyone was amazed and knew God had protected her. Rylan was glad she was able to be downstairs with the rest of the family so he could be with her. This had actually given the couple more time to sit and talk. They talked of everything, but mostly about God. This evening was no different.

After dinner, everyone retired to sit by the fire. The weather had turned cold and blustery, making everyone want to stay inside in the cozy room together.

Lanna, Scarlette, and Katherine were working on their embroidery, while Stephen, Stephen Jr., and the twins were doing other various things such as reading. The little ones played on the floor, beginning to grow sleepy. That purposely left Rylan and Brenna. Brenna sat in her usual spot of late, nearest to the fire with a blanket over her lap and reading her Bible.

Rylan had just come in to join them. He weaved through everyone and sat down in the chair next to Brenna.

"All packed?" Brenna looked up from her Bible and asked.

"I believe so. I didn't really have much to pack because I left home in a hurry."

"How early will you be off tomorrow?"

"Before sun up," Rylan replied. Brenna nodded and stared at the fire as he continued, "This will give you ample time to recover fully."

"It will be about March when you return, am I correct?"

"Yes. I'm praying for good weather so the journey will be sooner."

"Then we'll be married," Brenna stated excitedly. It seemed very quick, but then again, two months seemed far away as well.

"Where are you reading from?"

"Oh," she'd forgotten what she held in her hands, "In James."

"Ah yes…James. One of my favorites, 'Count it all joy when ye fall into divers temptations; knowing this, that the trying of your faith worketh patience,'" he quoted and gazed at the fire also.

Brenna couldn't help but recall Rylan's prayer the day of the accident. Even though she wasn't able to speak or barely breathe for that matter, she heard very well. She would never forget what he'd said. Any lingering doubt she might have had concerning marrying him disappeared completely that day. Two months was going to feel like an eternity for she was ready to marry him straight away. She couldn't wait until they could begin their life together.

"Would you like to read together for a while?" Rylan broke into her musings and asked. Brenna nodded happily.

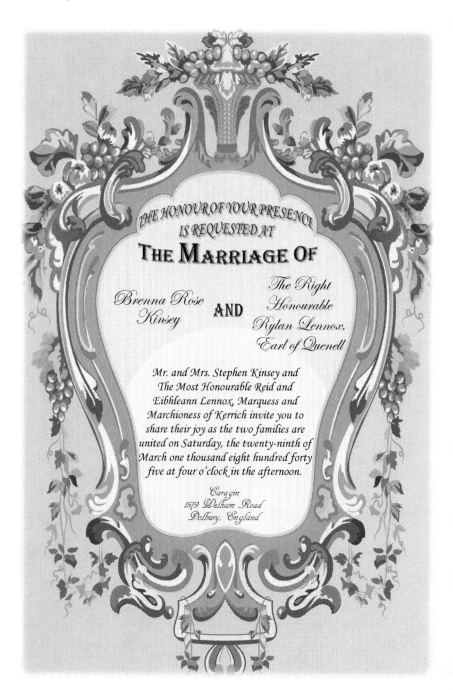

THE HONOUR OF YOUR PRESENCE
IS REQUESTED AT

THE MARRIAGE OF

Brenna Rose Kinsey **AND** *The Right Honourable Rylan Lennox, Earl of Quenell*

Mr. and Mrs. Stephen Kinsey and
The Most Honourable Reid and
Eibhleann Lennox, Marquess and
Marchioness of Kerrich invite you to
share their joy as the two families are
united on Saturday, the twenty-ninth of
March one thousand eight hundred forty
five at four o'clock in the afternoon.

*Caragin
1579 Welham Road
Dolbury, England*

CHAPTER FOURTEEN

March 1845

ord, will it be today? Brenna walked to the end of the porch. She gazed up the road and sighed. Nothing.

"Watching for him again?" Katherine came beside her and innocently asked.

"Maybe," Brenna glanced down at her.

"Don't worry, he'll be here any day now." Scarlette must

have overheard and also came over.

"I know…it's just been so long or at least feels like it."

"That's how everything seems to me…long!" Scarlette and Brenna laughed at Katherine's sweet attempt to encourage. "What?" She had no idea how cute she was.

"How about you? Have you heard anything from your gentleman of interest?" Brenna asked, referring to David Eldridge, who had taken a special interest in Scarlette ever since the Season.

"I replied to his letter only yesterday."

"Is he going to come and propose to you like Rylan did to Brenna?" Katherine asked. Her older sisters didn't even care to answer her silly question. Brenna chuckled, as a small pang of sadness came to her.

"I'm going to miss all of you when I leave for Ireland," she then voiced her thoughts.

"We will also!" All three young women embraced each other and tried not to cry. All of a sudden, Brenna gently pulled away for no reason at all and glanced at the road again.

I'm surely making it seem even longer by acting like this. She was about to turn to go inside when she heard something. Sure enough, a carriage slowly came into view. Brenna's heart quickened as she rushed to the stairs. A few weeks ago, Brenna might not have been able to run to meet them, but she was altogether healed.

"They're here! They're here!" Katherine began to shout for all to hear.

Before the carriage had a chance to stop for him, Rylan opened the door and jumped out. He couldn't wait one more second. When they neared each other, Rylan reached out and grasped both of Brenna's hands.

"I'm so glad to see you!" His smile and earnest tone melted her heart, "How are you? Are you feeling better?"

"Yes, so much better. And you? How was your journey?"

"Just fine, although very long."
"Waiting for you was much worse."

The carriage finished driving up the last bit of road and stopped in front of the house. By now, every Kinsey was outside and waiting to meet Lord and Lady Kerrich. After Reid and Eibhleann emerged and the introductions made, Eibhleann surprised Brenna by giving her a quick hug.

"I'm so 'appy for ya both…and to get to nu ya better," she stated in her Irish accent. Brenna was equally excited to learn more about Rylan's intriguing family.

"Thank you. I'm so glad you could come," Brenna replied.
"We couldn't miss it."

"Please, come inside," Stephen spoke up and they all made their way inside."

When Brenna felt the warm sunlight hit her face, she opened her eyes. She stretched and glanced out the window from her place on the bed. The sun was shining and there wasn't a cloud in the sky.

"A perfect day for a wedding," she sighed with excitement. *I should get up and get ready.* Brenna slowly sat up. As she looked around her room, she changed her mind and lay back down against the pillow. She couldn't get up just yet and face the busyness of this special day. She began to pray and thank God for all He had done. As she did, she couldn't help but think of her past. How she wished her true family could be a part of her wedding, but there was nothing she could do about it.

I will not allow myself to ponder on regrets and painful memories! Instead, Brenna started to recall her past in a different way. She thought about all the ways God had protected, guided, and brought her to where she was today.

"I'm getting married," she said it out loud to try and let it sink in and seem real. *Not just to anyone, but an earl! I'm going to be a countess and live in an estate!* As if she needed reminding.

Brenna was about to reach for her Bible when something struck her. A single thought made her freeze. It was so powerful, she knew it couldn't be her thoughts alone.

What if I wouldn't have been found in that trunk? But that wasn't the only thing. It was only the start. *What if I would have been treated like any other stowaway? What if Hephzibah hadn't been there?* "Oh Lord, You were with me…all the time." More thoughts came flooding in along with tears. "You were with me the night…she passed away." *If it hadn't been for Rylan, the constable, and the Kinsey's, there's no telling what would've happened.* "Thank You for keeping me and protecting me through everything…and for bringing me here…through it all. Thank you! I praise Your Name!" Brenna was overwhelmed with how good God was and how much He loved her. She remained there for some time in His presence.

Brenna finally got up and went over to wash her face when someone knocked on the door.

"Come in, Pensee." The door opened but it was Scarlette.

"I told Pensee I would look in on you and see if you were awake."

"Oh, thank you. Is anyone else up yet?" Brenna asked.

"If you mean Rylan, I don't know. I haven't gone downstairs yet."

"You know me too well," Brenna chuckled.

"Dear, you're getting married today!" Scarlette couldn't hold back her giggles any longer. They grasped each other's hands and very nearly jumped up and down. It was then, there was another quick knock on the door again. This time is was Lanna who opened it and came inside, but not before Katherine came running down the hall and slipped inside in front of her mother.

She didn't want to be left out of anything the older girls were up to. "Top of the mornin'!" Lanna greeted and gave Brenna a quick hug, "Are you excited?" she asked.

"Yes…very"

"Are you nervous?" Scarlette then asked.

"A little."

"Are you going to cry?" Katherine took her turn to ask and looked up at Brenna as if she would cry at that very moment. She quickly got her answer when Brenna met her gaze and laughed instead.

"I might eventually," she replied.

"I wanted to make sure we wud be able to say goodbye good and proper before everythin' begins and people start to arrive," Lanna said.

"Oh, I know! I wish we didn't have to leave so quickly following the wedding."

"Well, it makes more sense to stay somewhere in town for the ship leaves very early tomorra morn. An' we will all come for a visit pure soon, once you're settled."

"Good," Brenna replied and thought Katherine would be right about tears coming after all.

"We are all gonna to miss ya very much, but we're so 'appy for ya. Happiness alwus outweighs though."

"It's truly all thanks to you. If not for God bringing your family into my life…or should I say, bringing me into your family, there's no telling what would have become of me. I certainly wouldn't have met Rylan." Brenna sniffed. That was all it took to make everyone start to cry. Lanna pulled Brenna into another embrace. Scarlette and Katherine took the opportunity to get in on it and wrapped their arms around them.

"I knew there would be crying!" Katherine had to point out.

Rylan turned to look down the aisle as everyone on the terrace stood for the bride. He silently thanked God for everything He'd done to bring them together as Brenna emerged from inside the house and came into view. He'd never been so happy in all his life.

Through blurred vision he met her gaze. Brenna never looked more beautiful or full of joy as she nervously yet confidently made her way toward Rylan on the arm of Stephen. Their gaze was fixed on one another so that they didn't notice anyone else. Both of their thoughts were only on how happy they were, their future together, and how good God was.

Time seemed to slow as Brenna approached.
"Who gives this woman?"
"I do," Stephen proudly announced. Brenna gave him a swift hug before glancing up at Rylan. He reached out his hand to her, as he'd done so many times before in her dreams. Brenna couldn't stop smiling as she placed her hand in his, this time with assurance. There was nothing else she was more sure of. This was exactly what she was meant to do and precisely where she was supposed to be.

CHAPTER FIFTEEN

April 1845

re we nearly there?" Brenna's arm, linked with Rylan's, tightened with excitement. Rylan looked down at her, sitting next to him in the carriage, and grinned.

"Almost. Are you anxious to get there?"

"Maybe a little. How can you tell?" Brenna admitted sheepishly.

"Only because you asked the same thing only minutes ago."

"It's just been a long journey that I'm growing weary of," Brenna laid her head against her husband's shoulder and sighed. Though the travel had been long, she had cherished their time alone together. Because Rylan's father didn't make it to England often, he and Eibhleann planned to do some business there before returning to Ireland. Although his parents weren't with them, Brenna knew things would still change once they finally arrived. There was the staff, and Rylan would be working as well, taking care of everything and catching up on things during his long absence.

"It's only a few more miles," Rylan reassured, "And as soon as we get settled, I'll send for Colm Brodie."

"Oh yes! It will be good to see him…or meet him rather."

A little less than an hour later, Rylan spoke up.

"There it is, in the distance." Brenna sat forward and gazed out of the small window. A beautiful estate made of light stone was before them. It took her breath away as she took in the enormousness of it all. Several trees surrounding it were in full bloom and the bright blue ocean behind made the scene picturesque. It was more spectacular than she'd ever imagined. This was her new home!

How will I even know where everything is and what all the rooms hold? She asked herself and blinked a few times to be certain it was real. It was at least five times bigger than the house she'd grown up in. Brenna was speechless as they neared the outer court. Rylan, who observed her intently, knew she must be pleased by her awed smile and the sheer wonder in her eyes.

Brenna watched the beautiful gardens pass by until the carriage carried them by a gatehouse and into an inner court. In getting a closer view, she quickly noticed how large the bay windows of the house were. She then caught sight of about forty people standing outside of the entrance. They were dressed in staff uniform.

"Why are they all outside?" Brenna glanced back at Rylan in

confusion. Rylan briefly looked passed her out the window before answering.

"It is the staff."

"What are they doing?"

"They want to greet the new lady of the house," his face softened by a smile that made her heart melt.

Brenna suddenly became shy when the carriage came to a halt in front of the entrance. A footman walked up to the door, and Brenna meekly stepped out after Rylan. She was again taken back by the vastness of the house before her. She moved her gaze upward, wondering when the height of it would end! She felt the staff's stares as she self-consciously waited for Rylan to finish instructing the footmen where to take the luggage. He soon came up behind her and reassuringly placed his hand on her back. They began to walk down the procession line. As they passed each of the servants Rylan greeted them kindly by name and Brenna nodded.

"My Lady," each member of the staff responded and quickly bowed or curtsied. Brenna wasn't used to being called it. She was now a countess, but she still thought they were referring to someone other than herself.

They ended up just outside of the entrance when Rylan stopped in front of four people. Three men and one woman, dressed in more formal attire and not in uniforms like the others. Rylan shook hands with the men as they offered their congratulations. They then turned to Brenna.

"We are honored to have you, My Lady," one of them said.

"Thank you," she replied.

"Dear, these are my stewards, Eli McConahay and Paul Wilkinson."

"Nice to meet you both."

"My Lady," they replied and bowed in turn. Brenna guessed that both men were well into their fifties if not sixties. They seemed nice enough, but very business minded.

"Without these two, Saerlaith wouldn't be able to function."

"Oh, go on," Eli chuckled and waved him away. Brenna was a little relieved to see them relax a bit.

Rylan then turned to the other two standing nearby.

"Equally important is Mrs. Harrison the housekeeper, and Hughes the butler." The butler was a stout fellow, who was balding, with a decorous look on his face, and the housekeeper curtsied in a formal manner.

When the introductions had been made, Rylan glanced at Brenna, "Would you like to rest for a while and unpack some things or do you want to have a look around?"

"Oh, please show me around! I want to see everything."

"Well then, that's what we shall do," Rylan chuckled, "but not before this!" He completely surprised his new bride by lifting her into his arms with ease and carrying her over the threshold. The act caused most of the staff to laugh or giggle quietly. They weren't used to seeing their young master completely smitten and happy.

"Come with me, Lady Quenell."

"But of course, Lord Quenell," Brenna tried to mimic his British accent. Once inside, Rylan gently lowered Brenna then offered her his arm. They walked through the corridor and into a spacious room.

"This is The Great Hall." Rich dark wood paneling gave it a regal feeling, especially with a striking contrast of a white marble fireplace as the focal point. Brenna's gaze was instantly drawn to it. The family's coat of arms was mounted above the large mantle that had roses intricately carved into it. Brenna liked that the floor to ceiling windows didn't have heavy draperies to brighten the otherwise dark room, not to mention the beautiful view outside.

As they moved toward the opening to continue the tour, Brenna noticed a date of one thousand six hundred thirty eight carved above the archway.

"What does this mean?"

"It is the year that the building of Saerlaith was completed."

"Oh my…there's so much history here."

"Indeed. It's been in our family ever since. The Great Hall leads into the dining room. Before I was born there was a fire that destroyed parts of the east wing. The dining room, kitchen, and some of the servant's hall were rebuilt. Then over there," Rylan pointed to open double doors across the room, "Is the drawing room."

Brenna knew they must keep moving if she was to see the entire house before dinner. She would very well get to see much more since this was to be her home. The little glimpse she did get of the fancy drawing room was a soft greyish rose colored room with dark furniture. The light contrast to that of The Great Hall made it seem all the more pleasant.

"To the left is the kitchen and the servant's hall," Rylan motioned to a series of doors as they prepared to ascend the stairs. Everything Brenna had seen so far showed that even the smallest details were ornate and beautiful. Nothing had been overlooked in creating this magnificent home. Even the staircase had scrolled carvings in the molding and corner posts.

The view opened up greater from the next story. Directly at the top of the stairs they were met with another hall to the right and the left was an archway into another grand room.

"This is the library and leading off from it is my study. Now this room I know you will especially like," Ryan led the way to a door. The moment he opened it, sunlight came pouring through and lit up the hall. Again, Brenna found herself breathless. Rylan grasped her hand and they stepped in to what Brenna imagined heaven might look like. All three sides of the room were almost completely filled with windows. Sunlight reflected off the spectacular ocean view and came through the large windows. The light seemed to dance on the soft yellow ochre walls. With the light wood floors and white, almost pearl trim on the walls, fireplace, and the spirited plaster molded ceiling, the entire room was filled with warm, bright light. The damask fabric on the chairs and couches even matched the white moldings.

"This room is wonderful," she said in awe.

"This is The Ochre Parlor. It is my favorite room in the house. I especially like to come here early in the morning to read my Bible and pray." Rylan drew her closer to the windows, "You can watch the sun both rise and set perfectly from this spot."

"We could end the tour right now and I think I would be satisfied to remain here. I don't ever want to leave," Brenna's voice lowered as she gazed out over the blue sea.

"You won't ever have to leave...Saerlaith is your home now," Rylan, who was standing behind Brenna, gently turned her around to face him. "You've made me the happiest man alive." He then lowered to kiss her.

"Well, maybe I am a bit curious to see the rest of the lovely house," Brenna admitted once they'd finished.

"I thought you might!" Rylan laughed.

The happy couple strolled back down the hall and past several doors. Some were open, such as guest rooms.

"This is The Crimson Chamber, The Fawn Chamber, which belongs to my parents," Rylan informed as they went along. "Next is the formal dressing room for parties, our private family drawing room, and The Claret Ballroom." Brenna wanted to have a peak so they stopped for a moment. She was pleased to find another grand sized room with white plaster ceilings, matching trim, and fireplace. It was a tapestry room for the walls were covered with woven, whimsical designs. The room was complete with a huge matching woven rug.

"The tapestry was woven in Paris and the carpet in Yorkshire. During parties, which are a rare thing here, we remove the rug for dancing. The rest of the hall is more guestrooms ending with our chamber." They were going to keep going when a maid, carrying some of Brenna's things, passed by them and opened the door to the room. It caused Brenna's curiosity to stir so she followed the maid inside. The room had a rich feeling with dark blue walls and yellow accents. The large canopy bed matched in color. Brenna was delighted to see that the window overlooked the coastline.

"Where do those doors lead?" she asked when Rylan also entered.

"That one is another entrance to my study," he pointed to the closed door. "And through there is your dressing room and your personal sitting room. Your ladies maid's room is directly off of it." Brenna peeked in and found Pensee already unpacking.

"Hello, Pensee" she greeted.

"Allô Miss! Oh, apologies...I meant My Lady," Pensee smiled.

"No harm done." Brenna then rejoined her husband to finish their tour.

They walked to the end of the hall before ascending to the next floor.

"The third floor contains two wings separating guestrooms from the gallery. To the left are six guestrooms. You will come to learn that each room has a different name such as The Prussian Chamber, The Umber Chamber, and others I've mentioned. The Gallery holds portraits of past generations which I won't bore you with now. We might as well not go to the attic, for the only rooms are garret rooms. And that completes our tour," Rylan finished.

"You are a superb guide," Brenna sighed just as her stomach growled loudly, "Oh, pardon me!"

"It's quite alright. I couldn't agree with you more. I'm reminded that I truly dislike meals provided on ships and I'm ready for a fine meal!"

"Turn us again, O LORD
God of hosts, cause thy face to
shine; and we shall be saved."

Psalm 80:19

CHAPTER SIXTEEN

May 1845

ecause Rylan had to oversee something to do with a tenant, Brenna ate breakfast alone. She then got her Bible and went to The Ochre Parlor to do some reading.

She enjoyed her solitude for a little over an hour before she heard someone enter.

"Hello dear," Rylan approached the couch Brenna sat on. He

came up behind her, bent down, and kissed her before sitting in a chair across from her.

"Good morning," Brenna replied.

"Sorry I took longer than expected."

"It's alright. I've just been enjoying this marvelous room!"

"I didn't want to leave you this morning, but since you had fallen asleep, I took my leave. Are you doing better now?" Rylan asked, referring to her restless night.

"Yes, I'm sorry I woke you." Brenna had awoken from a dream. She hadn't meant to but she woke up with a gasp that in turn woke Rylan. "It was just so real."

"What was it about exactly? You mentioned bits and pieces."

"Well, it was a little alarming," Brenna said. She had been free from having them for so long she thought they were gone for good, although it wasn't the same she used to have.

"From what you've told me of some of your past, do you think seeing Colm, your uncle, could have brought this on?" Rylan asked in concern. He didn't like seeing Brenna disturbed. Even now, the look in her eyes told him she was still shaken by it.

"I don't think so…but I can't be certain."

"If it's difficult to speak of, you don't have to tell me."

"No, I'm alright," she didn't bother telling him that the current dream she'd just had was nothing compared to what she'd endured during the Season or before that.

"It was different than any dream I've ever had. You and I were walking in a field. It was one of Saerlaith's for I could see the house from where we were. The field was golden and flowing in the wind."

"Golden?"

"It was wheat, tall and ready for harvest."

"Wait…in Ireland? Are you certain it wasn't potatoes?" Rylan blurted at the preposterous fact.

"I know what I saw. It was golden." Brenna couldn't believe he was contradicting her dream! "Anyway, we were walking in the golden field. I don't know where we were headed, but when I looked to the left and the right, I saw we were surrounded by other fields, but not of wheat. It was green, but also brownish and horribly rotten. It even had a stench."

"Must be potatoes. That's odd," Rylan put in and leaned forward in his chair.

"I saw all of the other strange fields and began to wonder what was going on and where we were going. I looked at you and you just kept walking, staring forward. You continued on even when I stopped to look what was behind. Here, your parents, the entire staff, Colm and Laura, and other tenants I've met so far were walking along also. Everyone seemed like they were in some sort of daze until all of a sudden, a few of the staff turned and started to walk to the rotten fields. The moment their foot left the wheat, they vanished before my very eyes! I couldn't tell if something bad happened to them except the rest of the people walking with us grew terrified by it. Some were crying over their disappearance. This was only the beginning. Next, Colm started shouting because his wife Laura headed for the other field, but she wouldn't stop. He couldn't stop her and wept as he watched her disappear. And then…your parents," Brenna's voice filled with emotion as she relived her dream, "I ran to them and tried to stop them from leaving. I even held onto them, but nothing would sway them. I fell to my knees as they too vanished. Before it was over, I turned to look at you just as you began to go toward the rotten field. It was then I awoke." She sighed with relief when she finished. She'd managed to get through it fully.

"What do you think it all means?" Rylan finally asked.

"Well, it was certainly some kind of sign."

"How can you tell?"

"Because it was real…more real and stronger than any dream."

"But what can we do?"

"Plant wheat," Brenna simply replied with assurance.

Rylan wanted to try and be supportive of his wife, but this was absurd. She surely had no idea of how strange it would be. He'd never heard of anyone ever planting wheat in Ireland. It was unheard of! Nevertheless, how would he get that across to her without belittling her obviously disturbing dream?

Brenna was starting to catch on to what he was thinking when he didn't say anything for a time.

"You think I'm overreacting?" she asked and prepared herself for his answer.

"Well no," Rylan stood and walked to the window, "It's just that...I've never heard of anyone planting wheat here. The conditions aren't favorable to anything other than potatoes for our land and tenant's abilities. Potatoes are all they've ever known."

"What if God is warning us? What if something is coming? I don't believe it's a coincidence that I have a dream about the fields the same time you're making plans for planting. Just the other day you spoke of it." The moment she mentioned coincidence, Rylan was instantly reminded of his experience with the very word. He knew very well there was no such thing as coincidence. But was he ready to change everything for a mere dream?

"Does this mean no potatoes at all? Not one bit?" He asked. Brenna also stood to her feet and went to her husband's side.

"I can't know for certain. I'm not asking you to do this for my dream alone. I believe God is warning us...so we don't go along blindly, but to get our attention to seek Him concerning this matter." Rylan knew her words were right. Perhaps God was trying to warn them of the future for such a time as this, right before planting.

"Alright," he spoke with renewed purpose, "We need to seek God concerning this because we only have a matter of days before we must decide."

CHAPTER SEVENTEEN

London, England   *August 1845*

aughter could be heard, echoing down the street, as the three men stumbled out of the pub. They were kicked out for it was closing time.

"Goodnight fellows," a bar maid was also done for the night.

"Say there…what do you have planned for the rest of the evening?" One of the drunken men slurred as he offered her his arm.

"I'm going home as should you," she replied curtly, tired of dealing with men such as he.

"Might I walk you home, love?" This caused the other men with him to burst out laughing.

"What a charmer, George is!" they joked. The bar maid snorted at him also.

"I say, you can't even walk to your own place…much less offer me a steady arm."

"I'm fine, you'll see!" George looked at his two blokes and grinned shamelessly, "I'll see you two later!" he then chased the woman, who'd begun to walk down the street and took her arm.

"Bloody fool!" They shouted and jeered after him, but George only waved them away.

"Well, Edwin my boy…."

"Fred…." The remaining men turned to each other. Fred patted the young man on the back and tried to remember what he was going to say.

"I…which way do we go?" they both chuckled again.

"Follow me!" Edwin pointed down the street and they staggered away, laughing and carrying on.

"What else are you going to spend your money on?" Fred eventually asked.

"I'm saving up."

"Saving? For what? Sure doesn't seem like you're saving, especially tonight."

"Just saving, but with how well we've been doing…like the other night, I felt like celebrating," Edwin hiccupped.

"And that we did. Hey, are we lost?" Fred stopped at a crossroads. He leaned over to peer down each street until he almost fell over. Edwin stood still and tried to focus. He'd never been so drunk before or nauseous.

"I don't know, but I'm tired. I have to sit down somewhere."

They began to walk towards some crates on the side of the street for a place to rest. As they did, they couldn't help but lean on one another for support and began to hoot and howl, trying to sing the song from the pub. They hadn't the slightest idea of where they were headed, nor did they care.

"Here's a lovely spot," Fred stopped by some barrels and plopped down. "Whoopsie!" he laughed as he fell all the way back until he was completely sprawled out.

There were some trunks nearby that looked like a promising bed for the time being. Edwin lay down on top and draped his arms on either side. The last thing he remembered before either falling asleep or passing out was hearing Fred's loud snores, so loud it reminded him of his father.

Edwin slowly opened his eyes and shielded them from the light. By now, he was stiffly laying on his back facing the sky. He groaned in pain for his head throbbed. He didn't dare sit up for it would only get worse. However, his nausea swiftly told him otherwise. Edwin shot up, rushed over to a wall and threw up over the side. When he was through, he paused before standing up straight. He had to blink for he couldn't believe his eyes. The ocean stretched out before him and was moving past him.

What is going on? What happened last night? How did I get on a ship? Edwin's head ached with confusion. He couldn't do anything other than slowly turn around to take in his surroundings. Sure enough, he was on a ship! He then glanced to where Fred had lain. He was still sleeping hard. Why hadn't they heard the ship set sail? Why didn't the crew throw them off as soon as they saw them?

They have to know we're here, don't they? Edwin tried his best not to panic and to come up with a plan to escape, but there was no time.

"I see you finally decided to get up," a sailor, who must have been watching them, approached.

"What do you mean? You knew we were aboard?" Edwin asked without any respect whatsoever, not caring that he was at their mercy. All of a sudden, two sailors came up behind him and grabbed both his arms.

"Let me go!" Edwin struggled and watched two other men pull Fred from the ground and to his feet.

"What's going on here?" His bewildered look showed he was just as confused as Edwin.

"Someone tell the captain our two new crewmen are finally awake."

"What? I'm not working for any bloody captain!" Edwin shouted but was only laughed at.

CHAPTER EIGHTEEN

Saerlaith ~ Ireland

he moment Brenna dressed she went to The Ochre Parlor. She wanted to go to the best view in the house to see if the scenery had changed at all. A thick fog had come in from the sea three weeks ago and remained heavily over the area. It was so thick you could only see about a foot before you. It caused all attempts to begin harvest to fail miserably. No one could do anything in it.

Brenna, along with everyone else, was beginning to feel closed in. She'd been told that fog was all too common in Ireland, as in England, but people were a bit baffled with the last couple of days when a different type of fog surrounded The Emerald Isle. It was denser and almost appeared like a blue mist.

Brenna swung open the door to the parlor and walked to the window. To her delight, the fog was beginning to lift with the sunrise.

"Praise the Lord!" she spoke. She and Rylan had been praying very hard over this. Brenna could think of nothing else than to go outside and breath the fresh air.

The moment she went outside, Brenna took a deep full breath. When she slowly exhaled, she thought something was strange about the air. She walked across the veranda and tried to figure it out. It was more than just heavy moisture, but laden with a stench, like something was dead. The fog kept rising as every minute passed. Brenna kept gazing into the distance as she realized she'd forgotten her Bible that she planned to read outside.

Although, this strange smell makes me not want to stay out here much longer, she thought to herself and saw someone riding toward the house. It took a moment to recognize him as her husband. He looked worried but didn't say anything until he rode over to her.

"Is everything alright?" he eventually asked.

"Well…yes. Are you?" Rylan didn't answer he question as he dismounted and went to her. She didn't like his anxiety, especially since she'd only ever witnessed him as strong and sure.

"You were right," Rylan grasped her hands. He sounded stunned.

"What?"

"About God warning us…you were right."

"Rylan, you're scaring me. What has happened?"

"All of the potatoes from the neighboring fields, as far as we can tell, are lost. People didn't really know until the fog cleared this morning and they saw their fields. The leaves, down to the last potato plant are all black, and the smell is foul. Some of the men in town and I dug some up and they were rotten inside and out. My father has told me of other times this has happened. I even remember one when I was only a boy, but not like this. It's called the blight. We can't know for sure yet if everyone's crop is ruined...except for us and all our tenants."

"God protected us! He knew this was coming," Brenna spoke in awe.

"Yes, the wheat is unharmed and perfect." Although they were both astonished and relieved that they weren't affected by this horrible devastation, their joy was tainted in knowing the hardship that affected the rest of Ireland.

"All this time...having the tenant's plant wheat instead, despite everyone's criticism and ridicule, God knew."

September 1845

"Get them off my ship!" Several men threw Edwin and Fred down the gangplank. Edwin's palms burned from sliding against the rough wooden plank as he slowly stood. He looked at Fred, who must have skinned his face on it. He then glanced ahead to Ireland.

Couldn't have worked out any better, Edwin thought. Before now, he hadn't thought of how it could have turned out much worse for them after the trouble they'd purposely caused. He was tired of being told what to do day after day. He and Fred finally decided to do anything it took to put a stop to it, including thievery in which he'd grown accustom to. The only thing he hadn't counted on was being stripped of every last bit of money before being cast off.

"I'll not abide any swindlers on my vessel!"

"Well good! We didn't want to work for you from the start," Edwin quickly found his voice and shouted back to the captain. He and Fred continued down the remaining of the gangplank and onto the docks.

"You'd better leave here! If I ever see you again, I'll report you," the captain went on, but they weren't listening any longer. The young men had much more interesting things to think about as they took in the sights of this new city and delightful opportunities. The only thing that put a damper on Edwin's spirits was being stranded and moneyless once again.

PART
II

"Then spake Jesus again unto them, saying, I am the light of the world: he that followeth me shall not walk in darkness, but shall have the light of life."

John 8:12

CHAPTER NINTEEN

August 1846

r. Brodie to see you in The Great Hall, My Lord."
Rylan looked up from his desk at the maid's
announcement.

He came upon Colm standing in the hall, holding his hat in
his hands. Brenna was already talking quietly with him.

"Colm, what brings you here?" Instead of his usual bright
self, he was solemn as he urgently got to the point.

"I wus walkin' into town for work an' I began to smell somethin' awful. On me way I saw some men talkin' and 'olding somethin'. A wee bag of potatoes. It was Doherly, Kelly, and O'Sullivan," Colm looked down and gulped, "The blight has returned for a second year."

"Oh no," Brenna whispered.

"The sack av potatoes was all Doherly had ter show for after diggin' up ten ridges. The rest are moldy an' stinkin'."

"This could get pretty bad."

"What do you mean?" Brenna asked her husband.

"With all of our tenants doing just fine after another year of planting wheat, we might have to start being more careful," Rylan explained seriously.

"We could help some with our abundance. We have enough to spare," Brenna suggested.

"What do you think, Colm? Could that make things worse in any way?" Rylan glanced at Colm. All three of them knew the way Rylan asked advice from Colm was unheard of in their society. However, Rylan was far different.

"Well, from all you've told ter me aboyt the dream an' the Lord leadin' and protectin' us, then we nade to use what the Lord has blessed us with to 'elp someone else, to be sure."

"Yes, but mind who you tell," Rylan's voice lowered, "We don't want anyone's life endangered over this. People will most likely become desperate in a hurry. Some barely survived last winter. What's going to happen this year?"

"We need to pray for them," Brenna put in.

"Aye," Colm nodded.

"Then I need to discuss these things with my father and stewards—though I know they will readily agree," Rylan finished.

Efforts to ease the immense problems began in the following weeks. People were swiftly running out of food, the poorhouses were full, and with most landlords not relenting from collecting rents from their starving tenants, things were grim. Only a handful of landlords were lending aid with soup kitchens and purchasing Indian Meal, and loosening the strict renting dues. Unfortunately, the others didn't care or turned their backs entirely by leaving Ireland all together.

Brenna and Eibhliann had dedicated themselves to three soup kitchens they had formed with their abundance. Reid, Rylan, Mr. Hall, and Mr. Wilkinson had calculated how much they could give to help those affected by the famine, while keeping enough for their own tenants for the winter and possibly if the blight would last yet a third year.

More and more people flocked to their soup kitchens every day. So much so, Brenna began to grow concerned. With so many people, they could easily overpower them and steal the food for themselves. It was also getting difficult to see the poor state of some families. They were at the end of their rope and some had lost children to starvation. They had to start resorting to unspeakable ways to find food.

Brenna felt safe enough with several male staff close by. At first, she had thought it foolish for Rylan to instruct his dedicated footmen to accompany her and Eibhliann to the makeshift soup kitchens for protection. Yet, as things grew worse and people getting more desperate, Brenna was now glad they were there to assist.

It was almost impossible to close down for the day because crowds of people waiting in line for their rations was endless. She was in tears daily over the poor people of all ages who had been waiting in line for hours and literally begging when it was time to close. Brenna and Eibhleann would try to console them by saying they would return in the morning, but deep down, they knew some of them would be gone by then. It was heartbreaking. Children would grab at their skirts, crying along with infants and their helpless parents. They surely couldn't feed everyone in all of Ireland and themselves as well. This fact alone was the hardest to face.

Today was no different. The footmen did the best they could to escort the two women to the carriage.

"Please, me children…we've been standin' in line since before dawn. Please, could ya spare a bit of bread…just for me youngins?" A young mother shouted above the rest.

"I'm so sorry," Brenna choked in return and tried to quicken her pace. The woman's reaction to Brenna's reply was different from many others. Instead of continuing to beg, she lowered her gaze and tried to cheer her children as best she could. She was so weak, there was no fight left in her.

The last thing Brenna saw before the footman closed the carriage door was that family. The children's faces were green from eating grass. They were off as soon as possible.

Eibhleann and Brenna were silent except for their frequent sniffs from crying. Brenna wondered how much longer she could stand this. As they rode home, she caught sight of children on the side of the road digging through garbage, searching for food. Eibhleann must have seen her dismay and found what she was gazing at.

"Don't look outside, dear," she admonished gently. Brenna knew she was right. Usually she never did since hearing that there was a body of a poor soul, who'd passed on, in a ditch near the road. In truth, she didn't know what had come over her today. It seemed the horrible situations had finally hit her all at once. Seeing the filthy children on the way home to Saerlaith was more than she could take. All she wanted to do was be alone in her room and weep. She did her best to hold her tears at bay until then.

Once they returned home, Brenna went upstairs and was about to let her guard down and allow her emotions to flow freely, when she found her husband fast asleep in their room. He had been gone well before sun up the past few days overseeing the necessary things in efforts to assure safety for his tenants and to lend aid to the relief projects, as some people called it. It was a group of landlords who wanted to create work for the Irish so they could buy food or rations.

Rylan was no doubt exhausted. While Brenna readily understood, she still wanted to be alone somewhere, away from any prying eyes. She would have to ride somewhere and soon so she could have enough time to change before dinner was served.

Before anyone could see or question her whereabouts, Brenna slipped away unnoticed to the coach house. She easily diverted the stable boy with some excuse that made it sound as if a footman was going along. After all of that, she quickly rode away from the house and into the nearby woods. There she would be far enough from everyone yet still safely on their land.

She didn't bother getting off her steed as she began to weep over the suffering people, and cried out to God for help.

"Lord, we've managed to help them by feeding their stomachs, but what about the eternal value? We can feed them one meal a day but for how long? What about the long winter ahead? One meal can only last so long until they're starving again. What would profit the most is to show them…to get them to accept You as their Savior. They're so frightened of what might happen…if they die," she rode along aimlessly with blurred vision.

She had just begun to wipe her eyes and return home when she heard a noise. Out of nowhere, a man came running. He was running wildly, huffing and puffing, as if trying to escape someone. Brenna stopped her horse and watched him rush by frantically. Because he was in such a hurry, he wasn't watching where he was going and stumbled on something, causing him to fall behind a tree. Using the tree to lean on, he got up and immediately glanced behind him to see if he was being followed.

Brenna knew she needed to get out of there, yet part of her wanted to see what was going on and if she knew him. He looked somewhat familiar. He had dark, brown hair, wore filthy clothes, and hadn't shaved in months.

He almost didn't see her at all until he prepared to keep going. He then caught sight of a young woman. He instantly took in her wealthy clothing, fine horse, and her beauty.

There's no time! You have to keep going! They're not far behind, he frantically thought, his adrenaline still pumping. However, he didn't want to pass up this opportunity, especially since she was all alone.

Brenna tried to get a better look at him. Who was he? The man glanced behind him once more then approached her very slowly. She seemed to be in a stupor until he was nearly within reach. Then alarm suddenly awoke her. What was he doing? "Off you go!" he spoke and took action. Brenna ignored him and began to pull on the reigns to leave. What was she thinking? Everyone was currently dangerous! She now kicked herself for being so foolish and going alone.

He managed to move quickly. He reached over her and grabbed the reigns. The horse was starting to neigh loudly, spooked from the startling commotion.

"No! Stop!" Brenna tried to regain control of her steed, but it all happened so fast and he was too quick. He held onto the reigns with one hand and took ahold of Brenna's arm with the other. He could now focus his attention on her. Before pulling her off her horse like she figured he would, he strangely gazed up at her intently. She couldn't tell his thoughts, but it made her very uncomfortable. The look in his eye made her shudder for it seemed he could see right through her. She felt his hand on her arm loosen a little as if he was about to do something when she found her voice.

"Let me go or I'll scream! Someone will hear me, for they're right over —"

"Give me the jewelry," he blurted as if he'd suddenly changed his plan, "The necklace...now!" he shouted and his grip tightened. It was then that he saw the large ring on her hand.

"Hand over the ring too." With her free shaking hand, Brenna removed her necklace. He stared at her, unmoving the entire time. He finally released her, took the jewelry and shoved it in his pocket. When he glanced back up and motioned to her ring, Brenna couldn't help but hesitate. It instantly angered him. He knew he didn't have time so he reached for her hand. She started to struggle, causing him to grab ahold of her and rip the ring off her finger with great ease. She winced in pain at his roughness.

"Someone, help!" The moment she started to yell and scream out, the man tried to cover her mouth to keep her quiet. He didn't know Brenna would put up a fight before it was over. She immediately fought to break free from his hold and ended up biting his hand.

"Ah! You're not worth this," he mumbled and in one swift motion, he pulled her off the horse, while still not losing hold of it.

Brenna hardly knew what had taken place. She could only watch the man climb atop her steed and ride away without looking back. She got to her feet as soon as he was out of sight, gathered her skirts, and instantly rushed back to the house.

She nearly ran all the way back with a burst of energy that had come over her the minute her life had been in jeopardy. She emerged from the woods and found Stuart Young running toward her.

"My, Lady, are you alright? I heard shouting."

"I'm fine…I'm fine," Brenna replied out of breath. The terrified look on her face told him otherwise.

"Why are you all alone and without a horse?" Brenna was about to answer him when she looked past the footman and saw Rylan. He had come outside and appeared to be searching for her, for he scanned the yard where she often retired to.

He must have woken up and went looking for me…but no one knew where I was, Brenna felt ashamed at her foolish decisions and where they had gotten her. Tears stung her eyes at the sight of him.

"My Lady, are you certain you're alright?" Stuart asked again but was ignored. Her gaze was fixed on something behind him as she walked by.

Brenna couldn't stop her tears when Rylan saw her and began to run to her. She didn't know why she'd become upset all of a sudden. She wasn't hurt or anything. It was the realization of what could have easily happened to her by one poor decision. Brenna tried her best to calm down as Rylan neared for she knew it wouldn't be good for him to see her in such a state. He would think the worst and most likely be very angry with her.

Well there's no hiding anything now, she thought. Rylan swiftly embraced her, causing her to cry all the more by the safety in his arms.

"Where were you? What has happened?" he whispered in her ear. She couldn't speak right away. She knew this didn't appear good at all. Rylan was beyond concerned.

"I'm fine…really!" *Brenna, get ahold of yourself!* she scolded herself.

Rylan held her until she could speak further.

"I was riding in the woods," Brenna eventually began but couldn't look him in the eye. She only hoped she could tell him quickly before he could interrupt.

"Alone?" his cold, shocked tone made her flinch before meekly nodding. He said nothing more and waited for her to continue.

"A man came running by my in the woods…he stopped when he saw me." Brenna glanced up at him for only a moment. Rylan stared at her in apprehension, clenching his jaw. "He…." she choked.

"Did he hurt you? Brenna," his voice grew stern and a bit louder. She knew he wasn't angry with her as his face got red with rage. "Did he hurt you?" Rylan abruptly put his hands on her shoulders, causing her to gasp at his brashness. "Brenna, tell me!" he sternly asked again for he adamantly needed to get her attention and answer. Brenna still could not respond and only sobbed all the more. Rylan took her cries as a yes and turned toward the house, "Stuart! Thomas! Get some horses!" he shouted orders to some of his men, trying to keep his fury contained. He'd never been so mad.

"Rylan," Brenna finally found her voice again just as he was about to storm off, "It's isn't like that at all…he stole my jewelry and pulled me off of my horse." Rylan hesitated then left.

CHAPTER TWENTY

September 1846

renna woke up, leaped out of bed, and rushed to the chamber pot. She made it just in time before heaving into it. Once she was finished, she breathed deeply and continued to kneel before the pot just in case.

"What's the matter?" Rylan overheard and sat up in the darkness. "Are you alright?"

"Yes," Brenna slowly stood and went to the wash basin to

wash her face, "It was another dream."

"Was it about the land or wheat?" he asked, his voice groggy from sleep.

"No," Brenna didn't say more as she recalled the dream. She couldn't get the man from the woods out of her thoughts. His face was the last thing she remembered before awaking. She thought it strange, for in her dream he hadn't stood before her in the woods, but over her as he shut the trunk lid on top of her. Brenna suddenly gasped when it hit her all at once.

"What? What is it?"

"No…it can't be," she backed away from the dresser, completely stunned and covered in gooseflesh. *That's why he looked so familiar!* Now that she thought of it, she could easily see Edwin's face. He was the man in the woods.

"What?" Rylan asked. He was now fully awake with curiosity.

Lord, can it be true? "Oh my…I don't know how to say it! It's all so amazing!" Brenna sat down on the edge of the bed. Everything in her told her it was true. Her brother, whom she thought she would never see again, was face to face with her. "I don't know how or why, but the man from the woods…."

"What about him?"

"You're not going to believe me. It's too impossible."

"I can't if you don't tell me."

"Well…he's my brother, Edwin." Rylan almost got out of bed at her outrageous statement. Brenna looked at her husband. Though it was still dark, she could see he was taken aback.

"I tell you, it's true!"

"Why would he be here, of all places? And he didn't recognize you? Did he have a similar accent?"

"It happened so quickly and it has been years since he's seen me. We were only children." The frightening man, Brenna never wanted to see again, was now the person she wanted to find most. However, Rylan and the men searched for hours that day to no avail.

"You do believe me, don't you?" Brenna asked. Rylan opened his mouth to answer, but didn't speak. As preposterous and impossible as it was, he was quickly reminded of all the absurd things God had done in their lives. Even now, they were experiencing God's abilities by giving them a way of escape from the famine.

He did it with a dream, Rylan thought, *what if I hadn't believed her then?* That thought alone gave him cause to believe her. *Lord, I trusted You then...as I do now,* he silently prayed before he answered, "I do believe you. Yet, what good is it to find out now? He's long gone."

"I thought that as well. Only God knows."

They talked a little more before growing tired. Rylan said goodnight and lay back down. Brenna did the same, but she couldn't fall asleep just yet. She lay against her pillow, gazed up at the ceiling, and listened to Rylan's even breathing, still deep in thought.

"Lord, I know You gave me this dream so I would find out the truth, and I know You wouldn't reveal this to me only to never see Edwin again. Please let me see him again...please help me find him," Brenna whispered to herself. The man being her brother shed a whole new light. Now as she recalled his filthy and desperate state, it was a bit disconcerting. She spent the next few moments praying for her brother.

Before finally falling asleep, Brenna felt a wave of nausea. She sat up briefly, wondering if she would be sick again. For seemingly no reason at all, Brenna pictured Kylene, her mother, heaving in the same manner very frequently. Brenna was only ten years of age at the time.

Why, it was when she was expecting my brother, Benjamin. The thought caused a small smile to form on her face. When the feeling was gone, Brenna lay back down and closed her eyes. She only had wonderful thoughts and dreams for the remainder of the night.

February 1847

Edwin watched his smoky breath rise before him in the moonlight. He was breathing harder, along with his speeding heartbeat, now that his adrenaline was coming on him with what he was about to do.

He and Fred had found like company not long after being stranded in Ireland and facing starvation. The number of desperate men, willing to do anything, regardless of the consequences, was growing daily. Ever since winter had set in, every man was out for himself and his stomach. People were going as far as killing for the least amount of food. All the livestock were in danger of being slaughtered.

Edwin was so hungry, his empty stomach burned constantly. He and Fred, with three other men, had managed to come together to form a plan. They needed one another and the firepower one man supplied to carry it out.

The night they had been working towards was finally here. Fred gave Edwin and the others the signal that the coast was now clear for them to sneak up to the fence. The rich landlords had grown smart and kept almost constant watch over their precious livestock, that is, until the next watch was to start. Fred, the lookout, watched the stable hand leave to go and get the next man. This was their chance and they had to be quick about it.

Edwin and the others ran as quietly as they could up to the gate. One of them broke the lock and opened it. However, when it opened it creaked, causing them to cringe from the noise.
"Be quiet, will ya!"
"Be quiet yourself," Edwin replied. Their empty stomachs

made them all ornery and on edge. As soon as it was open, Edwin and three others crept inside the fence, holding ropes, and each tied it around some cattle. Their mooing and frightened groans made it impossible to be quiet any longer. Now they just had to be quick. The next person on watch was on his way.

"Come on you stupid beast!" Edwin pulled the resisting animal. Out of nowhere, a shot was heard. He didn't know what was happening in the dark so he continued to pull. He was through the gate when someone shouted.

"Stop right there!" The stable hand found them. Since Edwin was the closest one to him, the man pointed his rifle at him. Edwin had no choice but to drop the rope and freeze. He didn't have time to get the hidden pistol from inside his jacket.

The unsuspecting stable hand didn't know there were more men until Fred approached and shot the poor man from behind in cold blood. The stable hand fell face first in front of Edwin. In all the stealing and pickpocketing he had done, he'd never seen someone get killed. He felt sick inside at the sight of it. He glanced up at Fred, who didn't look the least bit shaken by just having killed a man.

"Don't just stand there. Get the bull and let's go! They're bound to have heard the shot."

"What did you do that for? He didn't see you. You could have knocked him over the head...not killed him!" Edwin yelled.

"What do you care? He would have shot you! I saved your life and that's how you thank me?"

"They're coming!" One of the other men shouted. Edwin and Fred saw lights quickly coming from the house.

Edwin glanced back at the dead man as everyone else ran for their lives. For the first time in his life, he felt truly scared and lost. He started to run for the trees. He would likely be shot at first sight. A cloud must have covered the moon, for it suddenly became darker. Edwin could barely see anything yet he ran all the more. He could hear horses and barking dogs gaining on him.

Unfortunately, he didn't see the ditch right in front of him as he continued on. By the time he did, it was too late. His foot caught on a stick and he went flying into it headfirst before losing consciousness.

"The light of the body is the eye: if therefore thine eye be single, thy whole body shall be full of light.

But if thine eye be evil, thy whole body shall be full of darkness. If therefore the light that is in thee be darkness, how great is that darkness!"

Matthew 6:22-23

CHAPTER TWENTY-ONE

March 1847

renna folded her hands and rested them on her protruding stomach. She twiddled her thumbs to get her mind off how long the carriage ride seemed, but it didn't work. She finally gave it up and sighed heavily as she glanced out the window.

"A little eager to get there, are we?" Rylan had been watching her and noticed her impatience. Brenna met his gaze and grinned.

"Perhaps a little. I just cannot wait to see all of them again."

"I'm glad they could be here and make it before our little one comes," Rylan reached over and took Brenna's hand atop her precious belly.

"Well, before we left England, Lanna said they wanted to come for a visit as soon as we were settled. I figured what better timing than right now, since I can't help with serving at the soup kitchen."

They drew near to the city on the coast when they saw a large group of people gathered on the outskirts of town.

"Rylan, what is going on over there?"

"Oh," Rylan took a look and instantly grew somber, "It's a hanging." Now Brenna saw the wood frame and the rope hanging from it as they got closer. "Most likely something to do with thievery...trying to steal food. I've heard of countless people killed over it during this winter. It seems no one is thinking straight these days. Starvation will do that, I suppose. I'm thankful our tenants haven't had to suffer thieves and robbers. We've done all the necessary precautions on our part but God is the true reason for our protection."

"It's all so horrible," Brenna sat back against the seat. She didn't want to see the fate of the poor soul. They could hear the mob yelling different things as they passed.

For some unthinkable reason, Brenna couldn't keep her gaze lowered. As much as she didn't want to see any violent sights, she had to glance out for only a moment to see who it was and if she knew the person. When she quickly looked out, the rope was just being lowered over the head of none other than the man from the woods.

"Edwin!" her erratic outburst made Rylan jump. "Edwin! It's Edwin out there...about to be hanged!"

"What? Brenna, what are you talking about? You know him?"

"Yes, yes! He's my brother. The one from the woods. My

brother, Edwin!" she shouted frantically, not knowing what to do.

"Are you absolutely certain?" Rylan gazed out as well. He saw a young man with the noose around his neck, being given communion by a priest.

"We have to do something," Brenna nearly stood up with how upset she was. "Rylan, we can't do nothing and watch him die! This is no mere chance that we came upon this."

He's about to be hung for a crime...a crime that must be pretty severe for death. Rylan was about to voice one of the countless thoughts flying through his mind, when Brenna looked at him earnestly, with tears streaming down her face.

"Please, we must do something...please!" she cried. Rylan glanced out again. If he was to do something, he knew he had to act quickly.

"Alright," he leaned forward and opened the door, "Donald, please stop here!" he hurriedly informed the driver. He got out but spoke to Brenna before rushing off. "I'll do what I can but you must promise me something. You must trust me. If your brother is about to be hanged, he must be dangerous. I need you to trust my decisions concerning him." As soon as Brenna gave a quick nod, Rylan was off.

"Lord, please let him not be too late." Brenna prayed and watched her husband run into the crowd.

"Let me through. Come now, let me pass," Rylan weaved through the people to get to the front.

"May the Lord in His love and mercy, help you with the grace of the Holy Spirit," the priest, standing by, was reading the last rites and Brenna had to shut her eyes with how close it was. However, her eyes shot open when she heard someone speak above the rest.

"Stop, stop right now!" Rylna had no other choice but to yell.

Edwin, who was closing his eyes, glanced up to see a man he'd never seen before, step up with authority.

"Who do you think you are…interrupting and interfering with the law?" the person in charge of the hanging asked.

"I am Lord Rylan Lennox, Earl of Quenell and I want this man turned over to me." Astonished whispers permeated throughout the crowd. Now that he knew this wasn't a joke, the executioner walked up to Rylan.

Edwin watched them speak quietly.

What is going on? Who is that? The next thing he knew was two men came to him, removed the noose, then led him off of the platform. "What's going on here?" Edwin looked back at the man. He was walking back to his fine carriage. "Who are you?" he shouted after him with no response.

"What happened? Did you stop the whole thing? Where are they taking him?" Rylan opened the carriage door and was met with a whirlwind of Brenna's questions. He didn't answer her until he sat down next to her and they jolted to a start.

"I was able to pay for his release. I'll have some men come and get him once we all return home."

"Oh, thank God you made it in time! I had to—"

"Brenna," Rylan interrupted. His seriousness made her stop. "What is it?"

"It's his sentence…he was caught stealing cattle and for murder." Brenna gasped in horror. Her brother, a murder? "We need to be very careful about this. That's why it's crucial that you trust me. I don't want anything to happen to you."

"Well, you don't think he would do anything to me. My own brother?"

"Look at what happened to you in the woods? And you said he locked you inside a trunk…you only being a young girl! There's no telling what he's capable of doing. He's a different man than the boy you knew." At first Brenna thought Rylan was too harsh, yet the more she listened, she knew he spoke truth.

"What do we do?"

"I'm not certain as of yet. We need to pray on this. All I ask is that you don't let him know you're kin. He might try to gain your sympathy."

"Yes, I believe you are right."

"We need to prove him somehow and see how much he can be trusted."

"Get in there!" The men roughly threw Edwin inside the small cell. He quickly got up and grasped the bars as the men prepared to leave.

"What's going on? Tell me what's happened!"

"I'd say you're very fortunate."

"Why?" Edwin asked, though he knew he couldn't trust anything they said.

"Naw," the other man laughed, "He's as good as dead no matter whose hands he's in...so don't be thinkin' you're free. You'll still pay for what you've done."

Why did I even ask them? Edwin thought as they chuckled to each other and left him alone. He had nothing else to do than face his loud thoughts, something he hated ever since the stable hand had been killed. Edwin detested the change that had taken place within him. His conscience that didn't seem to even exist had come alive. Although he hadn't been the one to pull the trigger, all the horrible things he had ever done finally caught up with him. So much so, he wasn't sure he was happy he hadn't been hanged. What was going to happen to him now? Would it only be worse? Did the mysterious rescuer have it in for him or want some sort of revenge?

CHAPTER TWENTY-TWO

 "And last but certainly not least, is The Ochre Parlor," Brenna stopped in front of the closed door and turned to the entire Kinsey family.

"What does ochre mean?" Katherine wrinkled her nose and looked up at Scarlette.

"Ochre is a color."

"Yes, and it's my favorite room in the whole house," Brenna finished.

"As is mine," Rylan put in and met her gaze. He had just

rejoined the group from a small matter he had to tend to. He could tell Brenna was trying her best to appear like nothing was wrong in front of her family, but he knew better. There was sadness in her eyes like all she wanted to do was cry. He also guessed she wanted to see her brother, whom he had just gone to see. He wanted to oversee where his men had put Edwin in the makeshift cell they had secured inside the gatehouse. Brother or no brother, Rylan didn't want to take any chances or have him anywhere near the house. And from what he'd seen, it only confirmed his uneasy suspicions. He could hear Edwin shouting and cursing as he had neared the gatehouse. He had never seen a young man filled with so much anger.

Brenna hadn't gotten a chance to talk with Rylan about it since they had met the Kinsey's at the harbor. Somehow he had to get through to her that whatever Edwin was like growing up, he was a different person now and no doubt a criminal.

Rylan continued to watch his wife open the door and laughed when her family immediately expressed their amazement and pleasure as they entered. He wasn't the only one who noticed something amiss in Brenna. Stephen, Lanna, and even Scarlette had caught on to it. After they had taken in the views from the beloved room, they all took a seat on various couches and chairs to gather together. They talked of the exciting plans of the new baby quickly approaching for some time until they all seemed to grow quiet at the same time. Lanna and Stephen were waiting to see if Brenna would open up.

"Well, I think I'll take the others to our rooms to get things settled," Scarlette stood, "That will give you all a chance to talk more." After giving Lanna a knowing look, she gathered her siblings and left.

"How is everyone fairing now during the famine? We have all been praying for the people affected by it," Stephen asked.

"As good as can be expected. More people are helping now.

Most of the landlords are shipping their tenants to America. God has been good to us and we in turn have been doing everything in our power to help the less fortunate," Rylan answered. He then caught sight of Brenna staring longingly out the window. "We've recently been enthralled with something else."

"Oh?" Lanna asked. Brenna instantly met their gaze. She was spellbound about her brother and nearly forgot she could seek their counsel.

"Dear, do you want to tell them about it?" Rylan asked and she nodded in return.

"It all started one day in the woods," Brenna began at the beginning although she tried not to let the story worry Lanna and Stephen. She didn't concern them with the few details about her life being in danger. By the time Brenna had informed them of the dream and the hanging just before meeting them at the harbor, they were beyond words. The fact that the last time Brenna had seen Edwin was years ago on the harbor in Boston and now they saved his life in Ireland seemed impossible.

"Where is he now?" Stephen finally managed to ask when the shock began to wear off. Brenna glanced at Rylan, for she didn't know herself.

"That's where I disappeared to. I went to the gatehouse to make sure he was there and secured."

"How is he?" Brenna asked almost in a whisper.

"He...well...suffice it to say...he isn't at all who you remember him to be, I dare say." Tears welled up in her eyes at this. Memories of her childhood were painful. Her older brothers had never treated her kindly, nor she them. This divine encounter was forcing her to face what she had worked so hard to forget.

Rylan looked at Lanna and Stephen as if again realizing they were in the room as well and watching their exchange in silence. In truth, they were still astonished. Lanna was praying under her breath. She knew this was the reason they were here, to help Brenna and her husband during this difficult and emotional time.

"I told Brenna we needed to handle this situation with much thought and prayer. Furthermore, I think it would be wise not to tell him that he and Brenna are related, but to see what comes of this. I believe we might find out more this way." Lanna and Stephen nodded their agreement to Rylan's view of the situation.

"He also doesn't want me to see him in my present state," Brenna put in, for she thought they would tell Rylan how silly it was. She was in the family way but stronger than her husband thought. *Why can't he see that?* she asked herself.

"I agree with Rylan, dear," Lanna spoke, much to Brenna's dismay.

"He's not going anywhere. There will be plenty of time to see him after the baby. Now I'll give you this...if I see some change in him, if he stops ranting and cursing with anger, I might change my mind." Brenna once again looked to see if Rylan still held their approval. She then sighed.

"Alright, I'll trust you."

Brenna turned over and opened her eyes. She glanced at the window and guessed it was close to sunrise. By the sound of Rylan's hard, even breathing, he was fast asleep.

I would have plenty of time to...no, I said I would trust Rylan. He told me not to see him just yet. She fought the temptation within herself, *I said I wouldn't see him...but what if Edwin doesn't see me?* Brenna recalled a small window into the gatehouse. *Harmless. And I take a stroll by there often on my walks.* That settled it then. Brenna quietly got up and tiptoed to her dressing room to dress.

The weather was still quite brisk but she barely noticed as she walked through the inner court to the gatehouse. It made Brenna feel all the more confident she was doing nothing wrong with the staff already at work in the gardens, preparing them for planting. She wasn't alone at all with the gardener, grounds keeper, and others about. They each nodded kindly as she passed, thinking nothing of her frequent early morning walks.

As she neared the gatehouse, Brenna briefly looked back at the house. No one was watching, so she left her usual path and stepped up to the small window at the back of the building. It was a bit awkward with her belly in the way when she stood up on her tiptoes to gaze inside. There, sleeping on a simple bed, was Edwin. She was surprised at how badly beaten he was. Under the filth, she could see bruises, cuts, and a black eye. She was too far away during the hanging to have noticed it the other day. With how peaceful he appeared as he slept, it was hard to picture him the way Rylan had explained. However, she knew he would never lie to her. She had seen her brother face to face in the woods months before and had gotten a good example of the anger in him then.

Brenna continued to stare at him when she felt a sneeze coming on. She turned from the window to cover her mouth with her sleeve but it was too late. The minute it escaped her, she heard Edwin stir. Brenna was about to carefully look in on him when his shout caused her to freeze.

"Who's there? What's going on?" Edwin didn't know where the noise had come from and figured someone was bringing him breakfast. "I know someone's there. Quit ignoring me and tell me what's going on! Where am I?" Brenna shrank away from the gatehouse when he started to shout and spew profanity. Tears stung her eyes as she walked back to the house.

Rylan was right. I should have never come. Lord, please forgive me for disobeying and not trusting Rylan or You.

CHAPTER TWENTY-THREE

"Mr. and Mrs. Brodie have arrived, My Lady."

"Please show them in," Brenna stood with excitement. Tonight was a special night for she and Rylan had invited Colm and Laura to dinner so they could meet Stephen and Lanna.

When they entered, everyone already in the dining room stood. Lanna could tell Brenna was quite excited for them to meet. Only a few days earlier, she told them of the amazing connection Rylan had made without knowing it before coming to propose.

"I'm so glad you could come tonight," Brenna approached them first and gave Colm and Laura each a hug. By then, the Kinsey's had come over. Brenna turned to them.

"I would like you to meet my uncle, Colm Brodie, and his lovely wife, Laura."

"Very pleased to meet ya," Lanna curtsied. She noticed a considerable amount of scarring on Mrs. Brodie's face and neck. She could tell Laura was self-conscious about it along with being shy, but she thought they were both very nice. Brenna then faced her aunt and uncle.

"And these are the blessed people who took me in. Stephen and Lanna Kinsey and their children, Scarlette, Stephen Jr., Philip, Andrew, Katherine, Tully, and Audrey," Brenna was out of breath by the time she finished.

"It's wonderful ter meet all of ya," Colm replied.

As they all made their way to the long table, Lanna caught herself looking at Laura. For some reason, something about her was intriguing. It wasn't only her partial disfigured features, but something else. She continued to think on it as the meal and conversation began.

"Laura, have ya lived in Ireland al' of your life?" Lanna finally got a chance to ask. She hoped in asking, she might find out why she was so interested in her.

"Aye."

"Do you 'av family that live close by?"

"That I do. Me mum actually works as a maid 'ere."

"Ah, yes. Maureen is a wonderful part of our staff here at Saerlaith. We're very fortunate to have her with us," Reid put in kindly.

"Thank ya, but I dare say she's the fortunate wan. Everyone treats her wi' kindness. She tells me it truly feels more loike family than a chore."

Lanna was glad to see her opening up more and more. Unfortunately, her questions weren't being answered.

"Is there anyone else besides your ma?" she asked and tried not to sound too nosey.

"I also 'av a brother...or 'ad one." Laura couldn't say more and suddenly became choked up. It made Lanna instantly regret her relentless inquiring.

Oh, now look at what you've gone and done, she scolded herself. Colm quickly came to her rescue and finished for her.

"'er brother was presumed ter be lost at sea when he went to go work on a ship years ago." Because she was so chagrinned, Lanna said nothing more about it for the remainder of the meal.

She made herself forget the whole thing until hours later when she was preparing for bed.

Lanna tried and tried to think of why Mrs. Brodie was of interest. Laura didn't appear familiar but there was something about her story and the way she had choked up.

Where have I heard a story very similar to what Colm had mentioned? Lanna asked herself yet again. She just lay back against her pillow when it came to her. *That's it!* She instantly sat up and tried to remain quiet since Stephen was asleep beside her. She was directly taken back to the conversation she'd had in a cold dingy cave when stranded nearly ten years before......

"Me da died av pneumonia an' a famine ruined our crops. I 'ad ter find a way ter support me family so I searched an' searched for a job an' finally got one on a ship. I worked for two an' a 'alf years before I went home. But when I got there, al' I

foun' were the remains av me home which 'ad been burned ter the ground. I foun' out later that the man who'd wanted ter buy the land that day 'ad gotten drunk an' started the house on fire in 'is rage...he said me mum and sisters were inside............"

The horrible scarring on Laura's face swiftly came to mind. *Could it have been from a fire?* Lanna was lost in thought. Could it be true? Was this Joseph's long lost family? Lanna could barely remain still now that she thought she'd come across something amazing. She knew she had to do something to let Joseph know.

Or at least just mention their names to him. There's nothing to lose in a harmless letter. She donned her robe, found some stationary, and went to the fireplace. She was no longer sleepy in the least.

"To what do I owe this surprise?" Rylan entered The Ochre Parlor to find a small table set up next to the window with breakfast served on it. Brenna was already seated and smiling at him.

"I thought we might have a private meal together."

"Oh? Is there a special occasion of some sort?"

"You could say that," Brenna replied. As Rylan approached and sat down across from her, she gathered her thoughts. It was indeed an occasion, but not an entirely lovely one. It was an occasion to confess. Brenna had spent several sleepless nights since secretly going to see Edwin. She knew she couldn't keep it a secret any longer. She hated what this seemingly little matter was doing to their marriage. It was lingering between them, something that had never happened before. Rylan had no idea but it was starting to eat away at Brenna. The only way to rid herself of it was to confess. It would most likely be painful to tell, but not as harmful if she continued to keep it hidden.

"I have something to tell you," Brenna finally spoke nearly halfway through the meal. "And I'm sad to say you won't like it." At this, Rylan wiped his mouth with his napkin, placed it back on the table, and leaned back to hear her out. It was pointless to stall any longer so Brenna just blurted it out.

"I went to see Edwin," she could tell Rylan was trying to contain himself so she could go on. She couldn't miss the anger in his eyes. "It was some days ago and he didn't see me at all. I merely looked in on him for a moment. Nevertheless, I disobeyed and broke my promise to you. I regret it greatly and I apologize. Please forgive me." While it felt good to get it off her chest, relief hadn't come yet. All she could do now was wait for Rylan's response. She cringed even before he spoke.

"Of course I forgive you…however," Rylan began. Brenna looked down at her plate, ashamed. "The way you speak of me…you make me out to be some kind of overbearing brute. I didn't make you promise to trust me for some sort of test to see if you would submit to my will. I'm trying to protect you from a thief and a murderer. It's going to take time and I knew you would be too emotionally involved to think of your own safety. You not only gave me your word, you gave it to God also." Brenna knew he was painfully right but when he mentioned God, it hit her deeply. She had told herself time and time again that she would keep calm and listen to all Rylan would surely have to say, yet her temper was swiftly getting the better of her.

It would be far different if he knew what I was really going though. How could he? He doesn't know what this feels like! Brenna was quickly becoming upset and couldn't keep quiet any more.

"What you've said might be true but do you know how hard it is? Here, my brother is on these very grounds. He knows where my family is and what has happened, but I can't even go and talk to him! How would you feel if it were you?" By the time she'd finished, she was nearly shouting.

"Do you honestly think if you went down to the gatehouse at this moment and asked Edwin to tell you everything that he would? No! Brenna, can't you see what you're doing? You're not trusting God at all. You're holding onto this situation so tightly you can't think straight. You're trying to make this happen on your own, when in fact, you haven't arranged any of this."

"What? Of course—" Brenna stood.

"Let me finish," Rylan cut her off, which made her madder. She angrily folded her arms and stiffly sat down again. "It was God who brought Edwin to Ireland when you thought you'd never see any of your family again. It was God that brought us to the hanging so we could save him just in time. The Lord has done just fine up until now because you've taken the whole matter into your hands and out of His. You're not in faith one bit," Rylan got to his feet and leaned his hands on the table to cause Brenna to look up at him. "If you don't give it back to Him, all of this is trivial and all for nothing. You've held onto faith before…don't let it slip away, not when we're so close," Rylan finished and was going to let Brenna have her say so when he saw her stubbornly set her jaw. He didn't want to quarrel or have anything more to do with it, not while Brenna was upset and angry.

"Until you have thought more about what I've said and given it back to God, we really have nothing else to say to each other," he turned, picked up the jacket he'd taken off and put on the back of his chair, and left.

CHAPTER TWENTY-FOUR

April 1847

*A*nd Joseph was the governor over the land, and he
it was that sold to all the people of the land: and
Joseph's brethren came, and bowed down
themselves before him with their faces to the earth.

⁷ *And Joseph saw his brethren, and he knew them, but made
himself strange unto them, and spake roughly unto them; and he*

said unto them, *Whence come ye? And they said, From the land of Canaan to buy food.*

⁸ *And Joseph knew his brethren, but they knew not him.*

⁹ *And Joseph remembered the dreams which he dreamed of them, and said unto them, Ye are spies; to see the nakedness of the land ye are come.*

¹⁰ *And they said unto him, Nay, my lord, but to buy food are thy servants come...*

¹³ *And they said, Thy servants are twelve brethren, the sons of one man in the land of Canaan; and, behold, the youngest is this day with our father, and one is not.*

¹⁴ *And Joseph said unto them, That is it that I spake unto you, saying, Ye are spies:*

¹⁵ *Hereby ye shall be proved: By the life of Pharaoh ye shall not go forth hence, except your youngest brother come hither.*

¹⁶ *Send one of you, and let him fetch your brother, and ye shall be kept in prison, that your words may be proved, whether there be any truth in you: or else by the life of Pharaoh surely ye are spies.*

The moment Brenna read verse fifteen in the forty-second chapter of Genesis; hereby ye shall be proved, it struck her. It seemed to jump out at her from the page. So much so, she even gasped. Was this the direction she so desperately needed? Now she had to finish the intriguing true story of Joseph's life that was remarkably similar to hers. The more she read the more she began to realize something.

When Joseph told his brothers he was proving them, he wasn't merely talking about their truthfulness to Pharaoh about not being spies. He was proving much more than that. He wanted to see if his brothers had changed and if they would give their lives for another, the youngest brother, showing their selfish ways were behind them. Brenna was persuaded that God was showing her something very important. Until now, she wanted to go to Edwin and ask him the many thoughts that consumed her mind the moment the truth was revealed. What happened the day when they locked her in the trunk? Was it Edwin's idea? Was it an accident or did they know they would never see her again? Did Theodore know the truth? Where was the rest of her family and why hadn't they responded to her letter? How did Edwin get to Ireland of all places and how did he come to the place where he could murder someone? All of these questions seemed to pile over her along with the hard things Rylan had said, weeks before. After her anger had subsided, she knew Rylan was right about everything. The chapters she'd just read about Joseph also confirmed what her husband had said. God had done it. He brought Joseph's brothers back to him.

Joseph never stopped trusting God and it all came together, she thought. "It was me…holding God back," Brenna blurted aloud. She was beginning to realize this only hours after her and Rylan's talk. It was only a matter of days before she had asked for God's forgiveness along with Rylan's. She then gave the situation with her brother back to God.

If I wouldn't have done that, I most likely would not have seen this in The Bible, she mused. She was now so thankful for what Rylan had said and that she heeded him. She was now able to be shown what they must do. As the verse said, they would have to prove Edwin, to eventually see through his wrathful armor. It would take kindness and time.

"Lord, help me be to patient," she prayed.

"Brenna?"

"In here," she called to Rylan. She was in their room, sitting up in bed, finishing up her time with the Lord before beginning her day.

"Good morning," Rylan came near and kissed her. Brenna could see by his smile and the glistening in his eyes that he was up to something good.

"Good morning to you also. What are you up to?" she asked.

"Well, God has given me direction as to how to move forward with your brother."

"Really?" Brenna chuckled.

"Yes, really…what is so funny?"

"Why don't you tell me first, then I'll explain." With that, Rylan sat down on the edge of the bed, facing her.

"I came to a verse this morning. Actually two verses. The first is the ninth verse of the seventh chapter in the book of Psalms. It says, 'Oh let the wickedness of the wicked come to an end; but establish the just: for the righteous God trieth the hearts and reins.' The next is the third verse of the seventeenth chapter in Proverbs, 'The refining pot is for silver, and the furnace for gold: but the Lord trieth the hearts.' I believe God wants us to test Edwin's heart to prove him in a way." Brenna smiled. She marveled at the way their Heavenly Father worked.

"So what was it you were amused by earlier?" Rylan then asked.

"He showed me the very same thing only moments ago."

"It's simply amazing!"

"Well, it's come about because of what you said. I know this direction has come because of it. It would only happen when I gave it all to God," Brenna said.

"I was beginning to grow concerned for you. I could see the situation starting to weigh on you. I've been praying you would see it as well. Anyway, this brings me to something else. I went to look in on your brother early this morning. He didn't shout or say anything. It seems the fight is gone from him at last."

There is hope for him yet! Brenna thought.

"My plan is, now that I've seen some change in him, to have him work with our staff outside. What do you think?"

"It's a wonderful plan!"

"Alright, I will tell him straight away. Would you like to accompany me?" Brenna's mouth dropped by his quick request.

"What? Really?" she sat forward with excitement when Rylan nodded.

"Now we mustn't let him catch on about you...not yet. I only hope he doesn't recognize your similar accent. Although, you did say you spoke upon your first meeting."

"Well yes, but it was more like shouting. It all happened so fast. I won't have to speak now though," Brenna replied eagerly before they entered the gatehouse. She felt butterflies in her stomach all of a sudden.

Edwin didn't move when they entered. He was sitting on the edge of his cot, gazing down at the floor, looking depressed. He didn't look up until Rylan cleared his throat. Even then, Edwin slowly glanced up as if he could care less.

"This is my wife, Lady Quenell," Rylan said in a business tone. He wanted to see if he would stand when he realized a woman was present, but he didn't. Edwin immediately recognized her as the one he'd come upon in the woods and had stolen from. She was now greatly with child.

I'm done for, he thought. Now he knew why this lord had taken interest in him. "I see now...why you've brought me here," he returned his gaze to the floor, "I attacked your wife, and now you've saved me only to get revenge."

"Think what you like but that's not it at all." Brenna thought Rylan's words sounded harsh until she reminded herself of

Edwin's hardened condition. She could reassure herself that she and Rylan were in perfect agreement over this.

"Sure it is. Why else would you save me from being hanged?"

"What I came here to tell you was, you are going to work with the staff today." Rylan did an excellent job of brushing aside his haughty questions and staying on task.

"You trust me?" Edwin asked incredulous.

"You'll start at nine o'clock," Rylan stated and walked back to the door, opened it, and motioned for Brenna to leave first.

"How can you trust me?" Now Edwin stood and grabbed ahold of the bars, "What do you want from me? Tell me!"

Brenna could still hear him after they shut the door and walked away.

"Again, a new commandment I write unto you, which thing is true in him and in you: because the darkness is past, and the true light now shineth.

He that saith he is in the light, and hateth his brother, is in darkness even until now."

1 John 2:8-9

CHAPTER TWENTY-FIVE

May 1847

ou can come in now to meet your son!" Lanna opened the door to the rest of the family and was met by joyous whoops and hollers from everyone. Rylan shot out of his chair, beaming.

"Congradulations, son!" Reid hugged him, followed by his mother.

Tears tempted to fall but he didn't care as he stepped into the bedroom. Brenna was sitting in the bed, holding a tiny but noisy bundle in her arms. She was grinning from ear to ear. Rylan meekly approached and carefully lowered himself into the bed. Brenna was glowing with delight along with appearing flushed and exhausted.

"What was the name you suggested?" Rylan knew he should know very well what it was, since they'd discussed it several times. It presently escaped his mind.

"Breckin."

"Oh yes. Where did you say you heard it from?"

"A story that was told to me long ago," Brenna replied.

"I quite like it," Rylan spoke in satisfaction.

"Breckin William Lennox," she stated and placed the little one into his father's open arms. Brenna couldn't help but laugh when Breckin immediately stopped crying.

"He has your striking features, I dare say," she said.

"That may be, but the small amount of dark fuzz atop his head promises to be much like your beautiful black hair," Rylan put in. He never did remove his gaze from the babe. They cherished a few more quiet minutes before Rylan brought Breckin out to show the others, for only women, other than Rylan, would enter Brenna's room.

A little later, Scarlette brought Breckin back to his mother. She placed him in her arms for Brenna to nurse.

"I'm so happy for you!" Scarlette sighed.

"Thank you. I presume this will be you in just a few short years, since it is official between you and David Eldridge."

"I can scarcely wait until the wedding plans are complete."

"Have you begun any?" Brenna asked.

"Cora, who is no longer avoiding me now that her brother and I are engaged," Scarlette momentarily stopped to laugh when Brenna rolled her eyes, "Anyway, she wants to accompany me to the dressmakers as soon as I return to England."

"I'm glad she's happy about the marriage. You and David

make such a handsome couple. I think Breckin has fallen asleep. Could you be a dear and get the nursemaid?"

"Of course," Scarlette left and returned with the nurse.

The second she took little Breckin from her, Brenna no sooner placed her head on her pillow when she could no longer stay awake.

The beautiful sunny day was too hard to resist. Brenna was tired of being cooped up inside so she decided to bundle up little Breckin. She got him settled in the fancy buggy, a gift from the Kinsey's, and went out.

As soon as they emerged into the refreshing, salty air, Brenna breathed deeply of it. She guessed that Breckin enjoyed it also, for he began to coo. She quietly pushed the buggy across the veranda, preparing to take a walk.

There you both are." Brenna stopped when she heard Rylan behind them. He covered the distance between them and kissed her.

"I didn't know you were still here."

"I had to finish a few things in my study before heading out," Rylan said.

"Do you think he'll listen to you?" Brenna asked. The evening before, while the entire family sat down for dinner, Rylan told them of a neighboring landlord. Because of his stubbornness and greed, he was having problems with his starving tenants. Instead of realizing they couldn't help but be behind in their rents, there was talk of the landlord planning to evict every last one of them. Rylan, along with Reid and Stephen discussed it and decided to pay him a visit to try and talk some sense into him to relent on his heartless and cruel intentions.

"I dearly hope he'll listen and not throw us out. However, I have great expectations in my father and Stephen. They've had plenty of experience in being able to persuade people by talking with them. If anything, we'll try to move him to at least pay for his tenants to board a ship to America," Rylan explained.

"Oh, I've heard the conditions during the journey are horrible for the already suffering people. They are packed into small spaces and many die before reaching it," Brenna said.

"Yet, most will likely die if nothing is done. I highly doubt Hawthorn will be swayed to do anything else, especially since he's been fairly lenient already during the past two years."

"I will pray he will be open to you."

"Thank you," Rylan quickly embraced Brenna, "You two have a wonderful walk."

"Goodbye." Brenna watched him leave then turned back to her son, "Alright Breckin, where were we?" she glanced down and spoke in a babyish tone of voice.

They slowly rounded the corner when Brenna came upon another scene. Gregory McKline, the head gardener, was instructing Edwin where he wanted something planted on the west side of the house. It looked as if Edwin had been planting a lot during this unusually mild day, for he was quite filthy from kneeling in the dirt. Although he also didn't appear to overly enjoy his job for the day, Edwin remained almost silent and listened to everything told to him. The two men didn't see Brenna right away, until Breckin began to fuss a little.

"My Lady," Gregory immediately stood erect. He then turned to Edwin, who was now kneeling on the ground. He quickly moved closer to the young man and nudged him. When Edwin glanced up and saw Brenna, he got up before she could interject.

"Oh, you don't have to get up."

"I see you and the young master are enjoying this lovely day," Gregory smiled. Brenna was still taken aback by how happy and excited all of the staff were over the family's newest addition. Most hadn't seen the baby yet, so Gregory gazed down at Breckin curiously with delight.

"This is his first time outside." Brenna paid close attention to Edwin's reaction. He said nothing but his gaze was fixed on the babe.

"So it is! May I ask what his full name is?" Gregory questioned.

"Breckin William Lennox."

"What a fine—"

"William?" Edwin blurted and surprised both Brenna and Gregory. Breckin chose this moment to begin to cry. Brenna pushed the buggy back and forth to quiet him. She didn't want to leave now. Something was going on with Edwin. The baby's cries only made him act more strangely.

"What is it?" Brenna slowly and carefully asked. *Lord, please let him open up!*

"Oh…nothing." When she thought it was over, Edwin continued, "It's just…his cry. It made me think of my brother." Brenna couldn't breathe! Was he speaking of Benjamin? "We had to leave him at an orphanage because he was sick. We had no food…his cries…." Edwin couldn't finish. Benjamin's screams when they took him away that day echoed in his ears. He didn't know what to do. He seemed to just realize that Brenna and Gregory were present.

"Well…a, if you would please excuse us, My Lady," Gregory McKline finally spoke when the silence was becoming awkward.

"Yes, of course. I'll be on my way," Brenna nearly choked as she continued on before her tears could fall. How badly she wanted to ask Edwin more. *Father, help me to be strong,* she prayed and fought to keep from pondering over the horrible thoughts of her youngest brother facing the same things she had inside the orphanage. It was one thing being trapped there herself, but Benjamin was so little and helpless. She could only pray Edwin would come to himself and tell everything so something could be done.

CHAPTER TWENTY-SIX

Augustine, England

e'll see you later."   "Take 'er 'andy," Joseph and Jake Harper rode together until they came to a fork in the road and had to part ways and say goodbye.

Joseph didn't have to travel much further before his home came into view. He couldn't help but hurry his horse along at the sight of it. This trip had only been a little over a month yet each time he returned home it was a joyous occasion.

Sure enough, someone was watching for him. Evan burst out of the house and came running towards him.

"Da!" As soon as he was to him, Joseph dismounted in time to catch his son in his arms.

"I missed ya."

"Me too, Da. And look!" Evan pulled away and opened his mouth.

"You lost another tooth! Every time I see yer it seems you've lost another. I 'ope I don't cum 'ome one day ter fend ya toothless!" Joseph teased.

"I won't be toothless!" Evan laughed. Joseph stood and glanced up when he saw Kalin now running to him and Audrey standing in the doorway, smiling.

"Well, looky 'ere. 'ello, my bonny lass!" Kalin giggled at this.

He happily made his way to Audrey, holding Kalin, his son's hand, and the reigns to his horse.

"Son, will ya take the horse please?" Joseph finally set Kalin down and handed the horse over to Evan. He then neared his wife.

"Hello," Audrey greeted warmly. She stood on her tiptoes and wrapped her arms around his neck.

"'ello dear," he replied before they kissed. "I see your growin' nicely," Joseph gently placed his hand over Audrey's protruding pregnant belly.

"Oh yes…a long way to go yet," she chuckled.

Once inside, Audrey went directly to the writing desk near the door. "I've been especially waiting for you…to give you this," she handed him a letter. It was informally addressed to Joseph and Audrey Brionny and it was already opened.

"What is it?" he took it and met her gaze.

"You must read it."

Joseph and Audrey Brionny   March 15, 1847
Augustine, England   Saerlaith, Ireland

Dearest Joseph and Audrey,

How are you and your beautiful family? I can't wait until both of our families can get together again soon. I apologize at the way I hurriedly wrote this. I've come upon something you might be very interested in, especially Joseph. Now, I don't want to raise your hopes only to have them dashed, but I feel I must inform you in case there is any chance it might be true.

I know we all well remember our time together, stranded on the island. One of the countless rainy nights you told of your past. When you, Joseph, returned home to see your mother and sister, your home was burned and you couldn't find them anywhere.

Anyway, currently I am staying with Brenna Lennox, the young lady I've told you about many times, and her husband in Ireland. Tonight she introduced us to her uncle and his wife. Over dinner I found out more about them. I didn't obtain her maiden name but her name is Laura and her mother is Maureen. Maureen works here at Saerlaith as a maid.

I hope this helps in some way. The Lord bless you all.

All my love, Lanna

Audrey watched Joseph's reaction as he read. He grew pale by the time he'd finished. He eventually lowered the letter as he glanced up at the ceiling and sighed.

"Is it true then?" she asked.

"Aye...thank the Lord! It's true so 'tis!" Joseph excitedly grasped Audrey's arms, crumpling the letter in the process, "We must go there...all av us...straightaway!"

"We have also a more sure word of prophecy; whereunto ye do well that ye take heed, as unto a light that shineth in a dark place, until the day dawn, and the day star arise in your hearts."

2 Peter 1:19

CHAPTER TWENTY-SEVEN

June 1847

dwin plopped down on his bed. He couldn't remember ever being so tired from putting in such a hard day's work. He had spent the day planting. Even though he felt stiff and sore and knowing the morning would come all too soon, it somehow felt good. For the first time in his life, he felt satisfied yet he would never admit it nor could he figure out why. All Edwin could tell himself was it had something to do with being at

Saerlaith and the people who lived there. The hard labor didn't seem so bad and the people in charge didn't lord it over him. Everyone was kind, almost too kind. Once in a while Edwin couldn't help but begin to despise it. All because he couldn't figure it out himself. The questions of why they had saved him and what they had in store for him was growing less and less as every day passed.

Edwin was quickly drifting off to sleep when he heard something at the door. It sounded like someone hitting the door with something hard.

"Who's there?" he sat up just as the door swung open. Because it was dark, he couldn't see who it was until he sauntered in. "Fred! What are you doing here? How did you find me?"

"Hush!" Fred scolded and shut the door behind him, "I came upon you yesterday in the fields. I waited until dark to come," he dropped the crowbar he used to pry open the lock on the door. "Well, come on! Let's go. I've come to get you out of here. The others are waiting for us." Fred huffed when Edwin didn't get up.

"Wait, what happened after I fell? None of the others got caught?"

"Ralph got shot...he's gone, but the other two and I got away. Time to go!" he turned to leave but stopped when Edwin didn't follow, "What's wrong with you? Let's go!" Edwin didn't really know what to tell him.

"You're not going soft on me, are you? It's got to be that. You can't actually like it here."

"I don't know. I don't!" Edwin shrugged and finally blurted in frustration.

"Ha!" Fred, getting quite frustrated himself, began to pace, "That is it! I can't believe you."

"Well at least I get enough to eat around here. Sure didn't get that being with you. They treat me decent. If anything, they saved me from the noose."

"I'm trying to save you right now. If you weren't so thick

headed you would realize it."

"Where were you the day I was almost hanged? If not for them, I would be dead!" Edwin shouted and forgot someone might hear.

"Bloody fool…they've gotten to you haven't they? You can't even see it. They don't care a thing for you. They're only using you for free labor. I watched you today in the field. They're using you!"

"How could you know that?"

"Because you're nothing special…good for nothing else but strength to work. They saw you, about to be hanged; they have money and now they have free work. Just test them to prove me wrong. Step out of line just once and see what happens. They care little if you live or die. Mark my words." Edwin only looked down, thinking about Fred's heartless, yet almost convincing words. "Well, I tried to warn you and give you your freedom," Fred tried his last attempts and backed up to the door again. When he saw Edwin still wasn't getting up from his spot, he sighed heavily. "Fine…stay. If you change your mind, here," he pulled a pistol from inside his worn coat, tossed it to Edwin, then left.

Edwin slowly lay back down and stared at the ceiling. For the first time since he could remember, he'd found some contentment, though everything Fred had said played over and over in his mind. Everything was up in the air again. He didn't believe it at first and didn't want to, but the longer he dwelled on it, the angrier he became. Were they only being kind to him because he was doing everything he was told? Was he only free labor?

Why, I'm no better than a slave! There was no point in going to sleep now. Edwin's fists slowly clenched as he kept thinking. He stayed awake all night allowing his anger and resentment to fester. He wasn't only mad at Rylan. It was much further back than that. His father, Theodore, anyone who had ever done anything to him.

By the time the sun came up, Edwin was in a state. He was exhausted and furious. He was going to leave and no one better get in his way!

Brenna never did get a chance to finish the wonderful story in the Bible. She had actually forgotten about it after she and Rylan gained the much needed direction concerning Edwin for the time being. Then the baby came along. So that night, nearly two months after first coming upon it, Brenna eagerly got into bed and pulled out her Bible after checking on Breckin one last time. Rylan was working later in his study so it gave her more time to read before having to blow out her candle for him to fall asleep.

Brenna flipped through the pages and found her place in Genesis. She quickly picked back up where she'd left off in the story about Joseph. Sure enough, Joseph did indeed prove his brothers through a series of cunning tests to see if they'd had a change of heart after selling him into slavery. He eventually, when much time had passed, saw their true character. They had changed. It was now time to reveal himself to his brothers.

1 Then Joseph could not refrain himself before all them that stood by him; and he cried, Cause every man to go out from me. And there stood no man with him, while Joseph made himself known unto his brethren.

2 And he wept aloud: and the Egyptians and the house of Pharaoh heard.

³ *And Joseph said unto his brethren, I am Joseph; doth my father yet live? And his brethren could not answer him; for they were troubled at his presence.*

⁴ *And Joseph said unto his brethren, Come near to me, I pray you. And they came near. And he said, I am Joseph your brother, whom ye sold into Egypt.*

⁵ *Now therefore be not grieved, nor angry with yourselves, that ye sold me hither: for God did send me before you to preserve life.*

⁶ *For these two years hath the famine been in the land: and yet there are five years, in the which there shall neither be earing nor harvest.*

⁷ *And God sent me before you to preserve you a posterity in the earth, and to save your lives by a great deliverance.*

⁸ *So now it was not you that sent me hither, but God: and he hath made me a father to Pharaoh, and lord of all his house, and a ruler throughout all the land of Egypt...*

¹³ *And ye shall tell my father of all my glory in Egypt, and of all that ye have seen; and ye shall haste and bring down my father hither.*

¹⁴ *And he fell upon his brother Benjamin's neck, and wept; and Benjamin wept upon his neck.*

¹⁵ *Moreover he kissed all his brethren, and wept upon them: and after that his brethren talked with him.*

Brenna was overcome with emotion by the time she'd finished. It was her dream to someday do the same. She dearly hoped Edwin's response would hold true to Joseph's brother's reaction. Brenna set the Bible down in her lap and prayed again, asking God for patience to wait for the right time to reveal herself the way Joseph had done. Joseph had forgiven his brothers but they were afraid for their lives at what he might do to punish them. His responce slightly bewildered her.

"*And God sent me before you to preserve you a posterity in the earth, and to save your lives by a great deliverance. So now it was not you that sent me hither, but God.*"

God had truly changed Joseph's situation around completely. Brenna thought of her own situation. Before now she hadn't seen it in the light of what she'd just read. It was true all the same. She too had been sent, it seemed, to preserve life. Not only their own and their tenants, but Edwin also. She saw how all the ways her brother's one act had affected. All this time Brenna thought she had completely forgiven her brother in her heart, yet now she knew it wasn't truly accomplished without having read these verses. Brenna needed to examine her heart and forgive. She now realized she didn't need to hear Edwin's side of the story or have it all figured out before making the choice to forgive or not. Though it wasn't as easy as she first thought or would care to admit, she made things right within herself and God.

By the time Breckin cried for his next feeding, Brenna had finally let go. She had turned it all over to the Lord and forgave Edwin entirely.

"…unto whom now I send thee, To open their eyes, and to turn them from darkness to light, and from the power of Satan unto God, that they may receive forgiveness of sins, and inheritance among them which are sanctified by faith that is in me."

Acts 26:17-18

CHAPTER TWENTY-EIGHT

dwin waited and waited. Finally, though later than usual, he heard someone coming. The man, who brought him breakfast, whistled as he drew near to the gatehouse. This gave Edwin time to hide.   "Sorry for the delay this mornin'. There were some problems in the kitchen," the young man didn't realize the lock on the door was broken until he reached to unlock it.   "What's this?" He pushed the door open and stood in the doorway, "Unlocked! But how? Hello…are you here?" Edwin waited for him to take one step inside then jumped him. He managed to hit him over the head with his pistol before the poor bloke even knew what was coming. Now that he took care of him, Edwin would have plenty of time to get out of there.

He went to the door and peeked out.

Splendid! He was as good as free. All he had to do was go through the woods to meet up with Fred and the others. He scanned the area one last time before taking off and he kept on running until he was well into the woods. The only time he slowed was when he heard a noise. Even then, Edwin didn't stop completely but only glanced back for a moment. Out of nowhere, he heard a gasp from a young girl. He didn't know what was happening for when he returned his gaze to where he was headed, he stumbled over someone. She was only half his height so he tripped over her and fell onto the ground. The girl was just as shocked as he, once he met her gaze. She looked as if she might cry at any moment when another woman was heard.

"Katherine, are you finding any flowers over—" Brenna froze when she innocently came upon them, "How did...." she couldn't finish. The young girl immediately got up, rushed to Brenna's side, and did indeed begin to cry with fright.

Edwin's gun had fallen out of his pocket in the process of falling.

"Just stay away!" he quickly reached for it and pointed it at them. Brenna pushed Katherine behind her much like Hephzibah had done to her in the alley. She feared that if Edwin got away, she might never see him again, much less find the rest of her family. She was afraid of that more than the gun pointed in her direction.

Katherine knew they needed help. She chose to bravely run to the rest of her family since they weren't far behind. After church, the Kinsey's and Lennox's packed a picnic to spend the last day together before the Kinsey's departure back to England.

Edwin barely noticed her running off and kept taking a step backwards. He didn't plan to stop for anyone, much less the lady of the house. He didn't realize the entire family was also there until Rylan and two other men came into view behind Brenna.

Oh no! Edwin began to panic a bit. He was sorely outnumbered other than his gun. At least he hoped the others were unarmed. "Stop right there!"

"Alright," Rylan slowed to a stop right behind Brenna and put his hands up in surrender. The other men did likewise. "You don't want to do this...just put the gun down."

"Don't tell me what to do! Stay away," Edwin's hand shook slightly.

"It's alright. We mean no harm," Rylan's calm tone irritated Edwin."We don't want to hurt you. We only want to help."

"Stop! Stop it!" Edwin shouted, "You just want to use me. You want to keep having me work for you. Well, I won't do it! I can't stand you. Blast you and your kindness! I can't stand it anymore. You should have let me hang!" he ranted. Brenna was about to breathe a sigh of relief when Edwin lowered his gun, but instead of leaving, he brought it up to his head.

"No!" Brenna yelled and took a step towards him.

"Brenna, stay away from him!" Rylan warned yet he couldn't do anything to keep her near himself without making sudden movements that might make Edwin do the unthinkable.

Brenna! Her name is Brenna? Edwin caught her name. He couldn't think straight. Was it true? Was she his sister? The last time he'd seen his sister was her horrified look when he closed the trunk over her. He didn't do or say anything for one thing was sure. *If it is true, then I'm done for. They have it in for me. It would have been better if I would've hung...anything but this!*

"Edwin, no!" Brenna ignored Rylan's cautioning and walked closer as she watched her brother pull back the hammer of his pistol. She didn't consider the danger she was putting herself in by going near him.

Theodore was right…about God's punishment. Thoughts flashed through his mind at the last moment. Brenna reached out to grab his arm when the gun went off.

"Brenna!" Rylan shouted as she fell to her knees. Stephen and Reid rushed to her side when Rylan did so. Only then could they see what had happened. Edwin lay on the ground and Brenna knelt over him weeping and calling out her brother's name. Stephen met Rylan's relieved gaze. He had surely thought the worst had taken place.

"Edwin!" Brenna cried.

"Thank yer an' 'av a nice day," Laura handed the package to a customer. They were just leaving when a man came through the door. Laura recognized him as someone who worked at Saerlaith, though she didn't know his name.

"Miss Brodie?"

"Aye?"

"Your mother, Maureen…she has collapsed. The doctor is with her now but she's callin' for ya. She seems to think she's nearing the end."

"Oh no," Laura glanced at Colm, who overheard.

"Go," he nodded solemnly, "I'll be along as soon as I can."

"Mum, I'm 'ere," Laura went to the side of the bed and immediately took her hand. Maureen had sweat on her brow. She opened her eyes and forced a weak smile.

"How are you feelin'? The doctor says yer 'av some sort of fever but he doesn't nu exactly what it is."

"I nu what it is," Maureen replied. Her voice was barely above a whisper.

"What?"

"Me time is drawin' near."

"No it's not. Mum, you're much too young."

"Now, don't argue wi' your mum. I nu...I can fale it. But it's gran' so an' you will be just fine. You 'av Colm and he's a good paddy." Laura didn't say anything. In truth, she didn't know what to do. Her mother became sick quite often. In fact, the day of the fire, she had been tending to her. Maureen hadn't always been like this.

Laura thought back, trying to find some reasoning for it.

It's been ever since he left, she recalled. Knowing that made her feel all the worse for she could do nothing to change it.

CHAPTER TWENTY-NINE

Edwin opened his eyes. He looked around the room to try and figure out what was going on and where he was. His face felt terrible as if burning. The last thing he knew was pulling the trigger.

"Where am I?" he finally saw Lady Quenell sitting at his side. Her eyes were closed as if she was sleeping until she heard him and gasped.

"Edwin!" she whispered, "The gun backfired. You're inside the house. Your face is a bit burned in places but you are alive, thank God." Edwin painfully moved to his side to sit up.

"Wait, you mustn't get up just yet."

"It's true then?" he groaned a little but managed to sit up with his back towards her. He couldn't bring himself to face her. "You're Brenna."

"You know?"

"It's why I was brought here, wasn't it?" Edwin was just figuring things out.

"Yes, though I hardly believed it at first. It was an act of God."

"Stop saying that," Edwin stood very slowly. He felt dizzy.

"Wait, where are you going?"

"I'm leaving, where do you think? You of all people don't want me here." He had just reached for the door handle when Brenna got to her feet, and rushed over to him, and touched his arm.

"Edwin, I forgive you…for everything."

"What?" Edwin's gaze shot to her. He now seemed angrier than ever. "How can you say such a thing? You don't know all I've done! You should have let them hang me," Edwin held his bandaged head in his hands, "I just want to die. I can't live with myself! Not after everything." Brenna was not about to give up on him.

"I truly meant what I said. I forgive you!" She then swiftly recalled the verse, "Don't be angry with yourself for God has turned it all around, to help save many lives. And just as I have forgiven you, so has He. All you must do is except it." Edwin covered his face and crumpled to the floor at this. It was the last thing Brenna could have expected to happen, nor could she believe the cries that came from him.

"I'm so sorry for everything," he blurted. All she could bring herself to do was kneel down next to Edwin, put her arm around him, and weep along with him.

It was some time before they could speak again. They were both spent and every tear had been shed, but great healing had taken place. In the midst of it, Edwin had asked for God's forgiveness. Since he'd done it, Brenna felt free to ask him if he wanted to make Him the Lord of his life, to truly be able to start anew. To her delight, he said yes and she lead him in a simple prayer. By the time it was all over, Brenna was overjoyed and Edwin did indeed feel new, filled with new life and free from any weight or guilt. He almost felt lost for he wasn't used to being free from himself. He had asked of the details from the time Brenna was taken aboard the ship in Boston.

When she finished telling everything, it was the moment she'd been waiting for.

"I've told you about myself...what about you? However did you get here and what of the rest of the family?" Edwin began to tell, though a bit reluctantly, from the time William found out the truth. He couldn't tell her about their father's current mad state, not yet. He would have to tell her gently later on.

"You mean to tell me, everyone is in England?" Brenna asked suddenly. She had to fight back the tears. Her first impulse was to want to leave for England right then, yet she told herself it would be soon enough.

"They're still there, working on the docks as far as I know. I left not long after we were given the job."

"You mentioned something about Benjamin?"

"Oh yes. He was sick...we were moneyless and starving so we had to leave him at an orphanage. Theodore told him as soon as we had money for food we would return for him. They probably did, long ago."

Brenna knew Rylan would completely agree with her to travel to England as soon as possible. Now that the whole story was revealed, she felt a restoring come over her. Now more than ever God was reassuring her that everything would be alright. All she had to do was keep trusting.

No one within ear shot of the sobs coming from inside the room dared to disturb them. Nearly an hour had passed when

Brenna opened the door. Rylan had been nearby in the hall the entire time for protection and support, not to mention prayer. He glanced up and watched the impossible. Brenna emerged first and was holding Edwin's hand. She led him into the hall. Though, they appeared drained from overwhelming emotions, Edwin looked like a new man, an almost entirely different person.

At first Edwin didn't want to leave the room. He couldn't bear the thought of facing Brenna's family after causing everyone so much turmoil. With some reassuring from Brenna, she finally convinced him to accompany her to dinner. Edwin was silent as they made the way downstairs. He fought feelings of being ashamed along the way.

The rest of the family was patiently waiting to find out the outcome of Edwin. When they saw them come into the dining room, they were shocked, especially seeing Brenna, holding his hand and smiling. Every one of them thought the same thing as Rylan did, that Edwin looked far different.

"Everyone, this is my brother," Brenna's voice grew quieter with emotion as she said it. Edwin hardly knew what to do. Saying she forgave him was one thing, but the way she treated him in front of the others astounded him. She acted as if he'd never done anything wrong. It showed him that it was all true. His amazement was only the beginning. He wasn't prepared for everyone else to treat him with respect instead of a criminal.

"It's a pleasure to meet you," Stephen approached him and shook his hand. The greetings only continued. Being treated like a new person helped Edwin eventually begin to see himself as one.

London, England

Nearly ten pounds. That's enough to pay for passage.
Theodore placed the money back inside the small box and closed
it. *Why, I even have enough for Edwin, if the fool would ever
come back.* Theodore didn't get up just yet to think further on
this. How long should he wait? It was hopeless to find Benjamin.
Should he and William return to America without them?

"Theodore!" William shouted and sounded as if he was
crying.

"Oh no…what now?" Theodore mumbled to himself as he
locked the money box and hid it under his mattress.

"Theodore!" Sure enough, William came running in from
outside. Theodore stood up and turned to him. His father was
quite upset and blood was coming from his forehead.

"What happened?" Theodore felt a little sorry for being
annoyed with him when he had truly gotten hurt.

"I fell and hit my head."

"What were you doing?"

"Just walking," William sobbed, his voice shuddered.

"Well, be more careful," Theodore got a rag and wiped his
head. It was deep but not too severe. He was beginning to wonder
about his father. He was getting worse it seemed. He was more
clumsy and childish of late.

CHAPTER THIRTY

*O*nce Joseph knocked on the door, Audrey turned to the children.

"Now you must be very good and not overly noisy. Your father is about a very important visit, alright?"

"Yes, mum," Evan and Kalin replied in unison just as someone came to the door.

"May I help you?"

"I've cum ter see someone who works 'ere. Maureen Brodie."

"Are you related to her?"

"Aye, I'm her son."

"Please follow me." With that, Joseph and his family was let inside by the footman. Audrey held the hands of her wide eyed children. They had never seen such a large home.

Joseph was very surprised to be led not to the attic, where the staff's quarters would normally be, but to the third floor. And not just any room, but a grand guestroom. He'd never heard of anyone in a lower class being treated in such a way, much less an Irish woman in an English landlord's home.

The footman stopped outside the closed room and rapped on the door very softly.

What is going on? Joseph and Audrey both thought. A woman opened it and spoke with the footman in low hushed tones. This behavior was causing Joseph to grow concerned. Something was obviously wrong. Was his mother alright?

Before Audrey knew what was going on, Joseph boldly moved toward the two people talking. It surprised her, for her husband was normally a man of few words and especially quiet around people he didn't know.

"Laura," he stated as if he was sure of nothing else. At first the woman, standing in the doorway, stopped speaking and froze. She was surprised that he spoke her first name. It wasn't until she looked directly at him when she gasped.

"Joseph! Oh my!" she covered her mouth in shock. Joseph and Audrey hadn't noticed the woman's disfigured flaws until she nervously kept her hand on her face as if trying to cover up something. Joseph became choked up with emotion at the sight of it, knowing all too well what it was from.

"It's a miracle! Oh Joseph," Laura hugged him and began to cry.

"I'm so sorry for everythin'. I tried to find ya," Joseph spoke. Kalin glanced up at Audrey and found her crying as well.

"None av that matters nigh. You are 'ere and jist in time."

"What do ya mean?"

"Mum is very ill. The doctor doesn't nu what so'tiz exactly. She thinks she's dyin' and I'm afraid I'm beginnin' ter think she's right for she's growin' worse by the day."

Joseph said nothing more and slowly went inside the room where Maureen was lying on the bed, with her eyes closed. He quietly approached and sat down in the chair next to the bed. He reached for her hand and held it in his own for some time, saying nothing. In truth, he was praying. Maureen eventually opened her eyes. She wondered who it was beside her. To her utter amazement, her gaze fell upon Joseph.

"My son! My son!" she slurred at first but became louder each time she said it.

"Mum, I'm here. I've found ya at last," Joseph lowered to his knees and leaned against the bed.

Everyone else stayed outside the room to give them time alone but they could hear their soft cries from out in the hall. There wasn't a dry eye among them.

"I'm so glad I cud see ya before I pass on," Maureen held onto Joseph's strong hand with both of hers, "I used ter be afraid of the noshun av dyin'. That wus before I saw a glimpse of it meself. I'll 'av ya know...I've seen 'eaven. It wus after your sister's 'usband, Colm, had a talk with me. He said I didn't have ter be afraid. I cud be ready ter meet my Lord if I did one tin'. 'nd I did it. I'm so glad I did," Maureen gazed up at the ceiling and smiled. "That was aboyt two years ago nigh." She was just going to ask Joseph if he believed as she when he took the words right out of her mouth.

"I 'av done the same. Jesus is me Lord an' Savior also." Hearing him say it was music to her ears! However, he wasn't finished. "Mum, I nu 'eaven is wonderful, but yer can't leave yet." It was more of a command and admonishment than someone who was grief stricken. "You're a believer...your time on this earth isn't over yet. Ya have work to do." Her son's statement struck her in a way she'd never thought of before. "There are so many hurtin' people out there with no 'ope…an' ya hold that hope inside ya, people only you can reach. Furthermore, ya have much more ter chucker in your own family. Ya 'av so much ter teach your grandchildren."

"Grandchildren?" Maureen suddenly asked. The more she thought on his words the more she realized that part of her had become selfish for thinking such a way.

She instantly began feeling better when Joseph quickly rushed out of the room and returned with his wife and beautiful children.

"For with thee is the fountain of life: in thy light shall we see light."

Psalm 36:9

CHAPTER THIRTY-ONE

July 1847

 dwin knocked on the door to Rylan and Brenna's cabin.

"Edwin, what can I do for you?" Rylan opened the door.

"I need to talk with Brenna for a moment."

"Oh, I will get her. She's just putting Breckin down."

"Actually, I need to talk to both of you."

"Alright, we'll be right out," Rylan's tone grew more serious when he saw that Edwin seemed a bit anxious about something. Whatever it was, it was more than a mere chat.

While they finished and got the nursemaid from the cabin next to theirs to look in on Breckin, Edwin walked to the rail. He gazed out over the waves. What he planned to tell Brenna would most likely upset her so Edwin decided it would be best to have Rylan there as well. He'd tried to tell her so many times before but couldn't. And now that they were on their way to England in hopes of being reunited with their family, Edwin was now forced to tell her before she would come upon it without warning.

Edwin took a deep breath when he heard them approach.

"Is everything alright?" Brenna asked as soon as she saw his somber face.

"Well, yes, in a way. I meant to inform you before boarding the ship but it pains me to tell you." Brenna glanced up at Rylan, who stood behind her. He met her gaze with a reassuring look. He then took her hand and squeezed it lovingly.

"What is it?" Brenna asked hesitantly. Deep down she knew Edwin had been keeping something from her. It was something that saddened him, which caused her to think the worst. *He mentioned that Benjamin was sick. Did he not make it? No, stop thinking like this!* Brenna fought within herself. She knew she wouldn't be able to bear what he was about to tell her like this. *Lord, help me...I keep my eyes on You. Thank you for keeping me in perfect peace.* A comforting verse was brought to mind and settled her.

"When we were on the ship bound for England there was an accident. Father was struck by a mast. The blow to his head made him unconscious for days. When he finally woke up...he wasn't right."

"What do you mean?"

"His mind. It was like the mind of a child." Brenna began to cry softy. She had pictured reuniting with her father countless times ever since learning the truth. Her hopes were swiftly dashed. She tried to hold herself together as best she could.

"And he was this same way when you left?" she dared to ask.

"I'm sorry to say, yes." After becoming right with God, Edwin greatly regretted how he had treated William. But it wasn't only his father, but every member of his family. "I am sorry," Edwin became choked up with seeing Brenna struggle.

"It's alright," she sniffed. Edwin couldn't take it any longer. There was nothing more he could do or say to help things so he slowly left. The minute he was gone, Brenna turned to Rylan and let her emotions loose.

"I'm so sorry, dear," Rylan wrapped his arms around her as she shook with sobs. He hated to see his wife in such pain. "I know this must be extremely hard to take in. However, he is still your father and he's alive. You can still reunite with him. Just keep thinking of it. You didn't think you'd ever see any of your family again." He could tell his words did bring her some comfort.

Two days later, England was sighted, although it seemed much longer to Brenna. The ship docked in the Port of London hours later. With the buzz of activity and chaotic unloading and reloading of the vessel along with countless other ships that lined The Thames River. It kept Brenna occupied just to keep from separating from her family and a few servants. They soon found and hailed an enclosed Growler Carriage and gathered all of their luggage onto it.

She didn't know how but through all the commotion and people, Brenna caught sight of something. A ship, only three down from the one they'd just come from, looked strangely familiar. She squinted to find the name of it and hardly believed what she found.

"The Hester?" she gasped.

"What was that?" Rylan had been directing the servants when he overheard her.

"The Hester! It's right over there!" she exclaimed as if he knew what she was talking about.

"The who?" he asked again. Brenna didn't have time to explain. Instead, she began to walk to it. Rylan couldn't very well let her go off alone. They might not find each other again in the crowds of people, sailors, and supplies of all sorts.

"Stuart!" he called to his footman as he started after Brenna, "Could you organize our luggage and send someone to arrange lodging for us?"

"Yes, My Lord."

Thankfully, Brenna wasn't walking very fast so Rylan caught up fairly quick. He was just coming up to her and about to ask where she was going and why when she started to speak to a sailor.

"Rob, is it not?"

She knows a sailor by name? Rylan asked himself in confusion. The sailor, to whom she spoke, set down a crate and turned to her.

"Aye?"

"I don't know if you remember me, but—"

"Ah! You're the little miss we found in the steerage! I couldn't forget that." Brenna smiled, though appeared a bit forlorn. "How are you fairing?" the sailor asked and took in her costly attire.

"Just fine. And you?"

"Good...good. Busy as always." Rob quickly began to feel awkward. He wasn't used to talking to refined ladies.

Brenna didn't know if she should say anything about Hephzibah to him. Yet, she was curious as to what had happened and if Rob knew of it. Although it was hard to speak of, she decided to gage his response.

"I presume it has been difficult without The Hester's beloved cook," Brenna intently watched his reaction. His face fell at the mention of Hephzibah just as she'd expected.

"Aye, we do. An awful lot. We miss her kind way, not to mention her grand cooking," Rob chuckled. Brenna couldn't figure out his joking tone and the light way he spoke of the deceased. Hearing him refer to her as gone seemed to solidify the truth. Her questions from not knowing what had happened to Hephzibah were settled at last. She silently thanked God for Rob because of his help. She then noticed him glance past her. She thought nothing of it until he did so again. She finally looked to see for herself and found Rylan.

"Oh, Rylan. I didn't know you followed me. Rob," she stepped aside to include the sailor, "I'd like you to meet my husband, Lord Quenell. Dear, this is Rob...."

"Rob Sullivan, ma'am," the sailor nodded kindly.

"He is part of the crew on The Hester, the ship that brought me to England."

"I see," Rylan smiled because he now understood.

Rob felt all the more strange to be talking with a lord and lady. Brenna noticed the rest of the crew, working around them, beginning to stare.

"Well, we don't want to keep you from your work. I'm glad to see you again."

"Thank ya for saying hello." Rylan offered Brenna his arm to leave when she remembered one more thing.

"Please send my regards to the captain and my condolences as well."

"Will do," Rob bent over to pick up the crate as they disappeared into the sea of people.

"Her condolences?" he muttered to himself when he realized what she said, "What did she mean by that?" When he stood up again, he glanced in their direction but they were already long gone.

CHAPTER THIRTY-TWO

uitin' time!" One man announced. Theodore set down the last barrel for the day.

"Alright, see you tomorrow."

"Aye."

"See you in the morning, bright and—" William set down another crate next to Theodore and cheerfully bellowed.

"Father, hush. That's enough," Theodore scolded him in embarrassment. He caught the other man laughing at them as he walked away.

"What? Why are you always cross?"

"Oh, forget it," Theodore sighed with frustration. He walked out of the storehouse and down the stairs. "Come on, let's go home," he called to William, who stayed put. *Still moping, I suppose...well I'm going without him then.* Theodore had just started when he looked down the road and saw a carriage drive up and stop. A man, who had a striking resemblance to Edwin, stepped out. *Edwin? No, it can't be. Not in fancy clothes like his,* he thought then continued on, *Sure looks like him though.*

"Edwin!" Theodore's gaze shot up to see who had shouted and saw William now excitedly standing at the top of the stairs. "Ed! It's Edwin," William met his son's look and tried to convince him.

"No it's not."

"But it is!" William persisted. Embarrassment rose in Theodore, especially when he turned back to the man to apologize.

"I'm sorry—" he stopped in mid-sentence when the man spoke.

"Hello Theodore."

"Is that really you, Edwin?"

"It is me."

"I didn't think we would see you again," Theodore was about to comment on his fine attire and ask where he'd been when he saw someone else climb out of the carriage. *Did he get married as well?*

"I brought someone with me," a smile broke out of Edwin's face. Theodore couldn't remember the last time he'd seen his brother look happy. "Our sister...Brenna."

"What?" Now he looked at her more closely. She had the same black hair and attractive features, though much older. "Brenna?" Theodore instantly overwhelmed with emotion, guilt, and a whirlwind of thoughts. He could do nothing but run his hand through his hair, something he did when he didn't know what to do. Was it true? Was it truly their sister they had believed to be dead all these years?

Brenna finally rushed to him and embraced him. He slowly put his arms around her to try and come to grips with what was happening.

"How can it be?" he kept saying, his voice wavering, as he looked down at her. The moment she glanced up at him, Theodore finally gave up trying to reason and accepted the truth. His guilt was too much for him. "I'm sorry...so sorry!"

"All is forgiven!" Brenna nearly whispered.

William had been making his way to Edwin, but stopped when Brenna had emerged from the carriage. Seeing Theodore upset, distressed him as well. He couldn't figure out what was going on.

"Father, come here," Edwin called to him but William timidly stayed put. When Brenna heard him mention their father, she gently pulled away from Theodore. She tried to keep her composure as she took in William. He was a sad sight to what she remembered him to be. He always had everything under control. A once successful businessman now stood before her with long straggly and ratted hair and beard, his clothes tattered and dirty, much like a reckless school boy at play.

The moment he noticed that she was coming his way, William gazed at the ground, folded his arms against his chest, and bashfully swayed back and forth. Brenna didn't want to frighten him with her crying so she tried her best to remain calm as she carefully covered the distance between them. One thing was certain as she prayed for guidance along the way, was that love never failed. All she could do at the moment was love him as she always had. She hoped in treating him the same way, like he was her loving father, might make him eventually realize he was.

Theodore caught Edwin's gaze, wondering if their sister knew the truth just as Edwin returned it with a reassuring, yet dismal smile.

Brenna hesitated a little when she stepped up to William. She was glad he at least hadn't run away. She considered if she should move closer, yet if she didn't embrace him she felt as if she might burst. Brenna finally made up her mind, went up to him, and wrapped her arms around him much like she'd always done as a girl. She couldn't keep back her sentiments any longer and began to tremble with sobs. She couldn't be sure but it almost felt like William slowly took her in his arms.

"Father, it's me, Brenna...your girl. I'm here and I'm safe...and I love you," she cried against his chest. William had a blank stare on his face, first with shock, then trying to resolve what was happening. His mind might not be right, but he had a big heart that went out to the mysterious crying young woman. He thought very hard about what she was saying. She had called him father, though in his mind it was the farthest thing from the truth. He couldn't be anyone's father when he was only a child!

"I love you and will never leave you again," Brenna just continued to love him with everything in her. "Papa, it's me! Don't you remember? You must remember...please!" she cried, begging him to recall their deep relationship. Her heart seemed to ache as she held him tight for some time before William suddenly spoke.

"Kylene...." he seemed to be surprised at it himself, not to mention Brenna. His head hurt with how hard he was trying to remember. Holding her sparked something within him. He pictured a woman very dear to himself, but it wasn't the one he held. However, it was Brenna's cries that caused him to think of another.

At first Brenna's hopes were lifted yet it wasn't her name that he spoke. She ardently wanted nothing more than to get through to him, but how?

"Kylene...." William muttered. *Her name was Kylene.*

"Yes, Mother. Kylene was my mother and your wife. I'm

your daughter, Brenna Rose. You've got to remember me! Oh, Papa…please! Come back to me," Brenna clung to him even tighter, willing him to recall. It was then William slowly pulled away. He put his hands on Brenna's shoulders to push her back gently.

Brenna feared he would leave, but instead of backing away, William lovingly touched her face. He gazed deeply into her tear streaked face as if searching for something in her eyes.

"Papa, I love you…I know you do as well," Brenna sniffed and tried to smile at him, fighting the constant feeling of hopelessness. She couldn't give into it by taking in his present state. Instead she kept picturing him as he used to be.

What is he doing? Theodore carefully watched William. He'd never seen him act this way nor stand in one place this long since the accident. William now gently held Brenna's face in his hands.

"I'm your Brenna…Brenna Rose," she whispered.

"Brenna Rose," he repeated what she said, "Brenna Rose."

"Yes, yes!" *Lord, help him…pierce through to his heart.* Brenna desperately prayed and dearly hoped he wasn't only repeating her words.

"Brenna?" he now asked, "Brenna?" William kept saying, first as a fact, then in questioning, and then he began to say it with more excitement each time. He put his hand on his forehead like it was coming to him. "Brenna," this time he assuredly stated, "My Brenna."

When Brenna was just beginning to lose hope by thinking it was only a game to him, that by repeating the name gained him some kind of attention. Nevertheless, this time his voice lowered and it held affection.

"You're my Brenna!" The more he spoke, the less his voice had a childlike sound. He sounded like a grown man, like her father!

"Yes, you're Brenna...my Brenna! You were lost. Oh, Brenna!" William took her in his arms as if seeing her for the first time. "How...how did you come back to me?" he choked. Brenna was overwhelmed with joy as she leaned her head against his chest. This time she was warmly held by him at last.

"God did it! God brought us together again! Thank the Lord!" she exclaimed.

"Did I just imagine it or did Father's mind just return?" Theodore asked in disbelief when he overheard William's excited cries and Brenna's joyous laughter. William had come to himself right before their eyes.

"Thank the Lord!" Rylan rejoiced from his place by the carriage with Edwin.

"Thank God indeed," Edwin put it.

What? Theodore was more shocked over what had come out of his brother's mouth than their father.

"Theodore and Edwin, my sons!" William and Brenna made their way over to them, hand in hand. William's astonishing behavior was far from over as he hugged both of them.

"Father, I want you to meet Rylan, my husband." A small pang of sadness hit William, reminding him of all he'd missed. He didn't dwell on it for long while the introductions and reunions were made complete. Having everyone together again at long last made it all the more apparent that one was missing.

"Benjamin...where is he?" Brenna suddenly brought up. She looked at Edwin, who was thinking the very same. He surely thought they had returned for him by now.

"He's in an orphanage. Theodore, let us go and get him right now!" William happily suggested.

"Father, do you remember?" Pain washed over Theodore.

"Remember what?"

"About Benjamin."

"Well, as I try to recall the last years, it's all sort of

unclear…like parts of a dream. It seems like you did tell me."
There was no use in hiding anything anymore. They all needed to
know the truth.

"Benjamin and countless other children were sold to a
factory of sorts but I have no idea where. I was told later that it's
a frequent occurrence there…however, now that you're here," a
hint of a smile formed of Theodore's face.

"Again, a new commandment I write unto you, which thing is true in him and in you: because the darkness is past, and the true light now shineth."

1 John 2:8

CHAPTER THIRTY-THREE

eston closed the door and was met with a wonderful aroma coming from the kitchen. He took a deep breath and went to it. He didn't have to go far for the cottage like home he shared with his sister was rather small. Nevertheless, it was cozy and ideal for them since Weston was only home for days at a time.

"I'm home," he quickly found Hephzibah bustling around in the kitchen.

"Oh splendid! Dinner is pure nearly done." Hephzibah loved to cook, especially when her brother was home. Weston took off his hat and coat then sat down at the table.

The minutes passed quickly as they talked about what they had been up to since seeing each other last. Hephzibah set the main dish on the table and sat down across from her brother. Weston waited until grace was said before revealing the interesting news.

"Rob saw someone today."

"Oh?" Hephzibah asked between bites.

"It was a Miss Brenna." Weston's sister nearly dropped her fork the moment he said it.

"She's alive? Theur spoke wif her?"

"Not I personally. She was in the harbor and saw Rob."

"Praise the Lord!" Hephzibah exclaimed joy.

When Weston and some of the crew had come upon Hephzibah in the alley, left for dead, they carried her to safety and got her the necessary help, but Brenna was nowhere to be found. Hephzibah had spent most of her time, while slowly recovering, greatly concerned for the beloved little girl and of her whereabouts. She prayed and prayed until she almost grew sick with worry.

"How I wish I would 'av bin there," Hephzibah sniffed and pulled a handkerchief from the pocket of her apron.

"Maybe so, yet just look at how amazin' it was to find out she's alive. That's why I wanted to tell you...to give you hope."

"Oh my...this is sa wonderful! Did Rob find out more abaht her?" Hephzibah stood with excitement and began to pace.

"Hephzibah," Weston spoke up but was ignored.

"Where is she stayin'? What 'appened that neeght?" Is she alright? Wot of 'er family?"

"Hephzibah," Weston stood to his feet when his sister suddenly stopped ranting and started to cry. "Come and sit dahn," he gently took her arm and led her back to the table.

"I'm sorry...I'm just so 'appy ta kna she's alive and well. I've worried about 'er fa so long." Weston knew she would react this way. He almost didn't want to tell her about it at all because he didn't want to upset her. She had taken the whole incident upon herself and blamed herself for it. All she was consumed with was that she had broken her promise to the girl about helping her get home to her family. Hephzibah's recovery was even slowed because of her worried state. Weston finally decided to tell her in hopes of bringing her some comfort.

"I know you're 'appy to find this out…yet, I think…." Weston struggled to find the right words when a powerful recollection came to mind. "Let me tell you abaht somethin' that happened this last voyage. It was durin' the dog watch and we were rollin' steadily with a strong wind having sprung up from the southward. There was some trouble with the gaff topsail so two men, Rigby and Stanton, went up to repair it. Somethin' went wrong and they both fell overboard. Because of the winds and how dark it was, no one saw it happen."

"Goodness! That is 'orrible!" Hephzibah gasped for she knew all too well that if someone fell overboard they were as good as dead for no one could save them nor could the ship turn back.

"The next morn we realized what had taken place. When the men fell they were able to grab ahold of a rope. To our amazement, Rigby was still hangin' on."

"It's a roight miracle!"

"We were able to pull him in. There was no way he could 'ave held on through the noight. He had to have been exhausted, not to mention the cold temperatures. When we got 'im in the ship he was able to stand and was coherent. Needless to say, everyone wanted to know how he had lived through it. Rigby said he couldn't have held on for long so instead of holdin' onto the rope he wrapped it around himself and tied it. He didn't hold onto the rope at all. The rope held onto him."

"What happened to Stanton?"

"Rigby kept tellin' 'im to tie himself to it as well but he wouldn't…he only 'eld on so long before he gave out."

"What a cryin' shame," Hephzibah sighed.

"In a way, you have done the same as Stanton." Weston knew this would get her attention.

"Wot?" Hephzibah asked, startled.

"This matter with Brenna. You've taken it solely upon yourself...worryin' on so. You are tryin' to fix it yourself and holding onto the rope with all your might instead of trustin' in the rope. It's as the scriptures says, 'be strong in the Lord and in the power of His might.' Be strong in the power of His might, not your might. If you're to truly trust in Him, you must let go of trying to fix it yerself and trust in Him to take care of Brenna. Hold onto the Father by faith." Weston knew his words must have sounded harsh but it was high time that she heard it. She was hurting herself the way she was going on.

The room was quiet for a while before either of them spoke.

"You know...you're roight. I 'ave been takin' this all on me. I need ta give this all to Him sa He can take care of it. Worry ties His 'ands from doin' any bloody good. Oh Weston, I'm sa glad ya told me this. Moight we pray together so I can give it to Him again?"

"Aye," Weston ardently agreed. It was as if a weight had instantly come off of Hephzibah. She had taken it amazingly well and Weston silently thanked God for it.

"Mr. Thordon, someone to see you."

"Who is it?"

"Lord Quenell. I told him to wait in the hall," the maid moved to the door, stopped, then hurried back inside his office, "Sir, I told them to wait in the hall...I tried my best!"

"What are you talking about?" Mr. Thordon shot out of his chair when seven people barged into his office, one of which was a constable.

"What is the meaning of this?" he asked, completely startled. He instantly got the impression of their wealth by some of their clothing, though more apparent than anything was how stern and angry they seemed.

"Wolsey, what are you doing here?" Mr. Thordon barked when he spotted his groundskeeper among them. Before he could answer, Rylan stepped up to the desk.

"I am Lord Quenell. Nearly two years ago, my wife's brother was put into your care. Shortly after Mr. Dorcet here," he motioned to Theodore, "Came to look in on him, he was not allowed to see the boy and was more or less kicked out. We have reason to believe, by a very reliable source, that you have been selling children to a factory for a substantial sum. We have come for you to take us there where we will retrieve the child immediately." Mr. Thordon was at a loss for words. He tried to come up with something but only ended up stuttering.

"I…well…uh…that is preposterous! Where did you get this information? I demand to know!"

"Sir," the constable stepped in, "You are in no position to demand anything."

"Excuse me?"

"You will take us to this factory, escort us in fact," Rylan finished calmly.

"First of all, I have no idea of what you speak of. All of the children are perfectly safe here in this building. Second of all, why should I? You have no—" The constable must have heard quite enough because he said nothing more as he went to Mr. Thordon and handcuffed him. "Unhand me! You can't do this…if what you say was true, I wouldn't tell you nor show you anything!" No one paid him any more attention and went to the filing cabinets to start searching Mr. Thordon's bookkeeping for the name of the factory.

The carriage came to a halt in front of a grey, cold building with tall bars surrounding it. Because theirs was one of three carriages, it caused a stir among some of the people within the prison like factory. A few, mostly children as young as five years of age, approached the bars and grasped onto them to watch. Brenna's eyes filled with tears as she looked at all of them.

"I want you to stay here, only because we don't know how willing they will be to unhand him," Rylan spoke.

"Alright. Oh, Rylan…look at all of the poor children. You do think he's alright, don't you?" Right when she said it she knew it was wrong to speak such doubt. Rylan knew it also.

"God has brought us this far and has restored your family. Don't start to fret now."

"You are right. I'm sorry. Perhaps we should pray before you go." Brenna suggested and Rylan grasped her hands.

"Lord, we thank You for everything You've done and what You are doing in this family. We pray for favor with the owners of this place and that they will give Benjamin up without question."

"And that everyone will be kept safe in the process, in Jesus' Name, amen." Brenna felt better already as Rylan kissed her and left.

By faith, Brenna continued to thank God for answering their prayers and watched Rylan meet up with her father, brothers, Wosley, the begrudging Mr. Thordon, and several constables. The one who had accompanied them to the orphanage had gotten others to come along for back up. They went in together. Brenna squinted her eyes to get a better look at the children behind the bars, trying to distinguish any as her brother. She knew it to be impossible since he'd only been an infant the last time she'd laid eyes on him.

It seemed like an eternity while she waited.

"Finally!" she breathed when she saw movement at the doors. Everyone who emerged was empty handed. *Rylan, Edwin, Theodore…where is he?"* Brenna remained at the window unmoving and holding her breath. The last one out was William. *Oh, no,* her heart sank but then she caught sight of someone else. Brenna gasped when she saw a boy holding William's hand. That was all it took to keep Brenna from remaining still any longer. She flew to the door, swung it open, and jumped out.

"You did it! Oh, thank the Lord! What about the other children?" she asked as the men closed the gate behind them.

"We got your brother without any questions with Thordon's help," Rylan nodded in his direction. Mr. Thordon's head was hung in defeat as he was taken to one of the other carriages. "Though it will take time for the rest, the constables are going to look into this further and get the orphans out of there."

Benjamin was filthy, wore tattered clothes, and was terribly skinny. He looked overworked and exhausted, but overall, he was unharmed.

"He knew us immediately!" William happily announced, still holding hands with the youngster. Theodore and William feared that over two years was too long for Benjamin to remember them, especially since he'd only been four years of age when they were forced to leave him.

"One of the first things he mentioned was the fact that Father's mind had been found," Edwin put in.

Benjamin glanced at all of them and smiled. He still wondered who the man and woman were. He finally tugged at William's hand and whispered.

"Who are they?"

"Why, that is your sister, Brenna. You don't remember her because she…went away when you were a baby." Again, the pang hit him with sad memories.

As Brenna went to Benjamin, knelt down to get acquainted, she couldn't help but notice Theodore's face. He was standing close by. Since reuniting with him only days before, she noticed a heaviness over him. It was as if he was weighed down by many things. This was the first time he seemed better. She figured it had been beyond stressful all this time. She wondered if, now that they were altogether, he probably thought all his troubles were behind him. Only Brenna knew he would never be completely free from his past until he gave his life to the Lord. She knew first hand that it made all the difference in the world to truly be at peace and filled with renewed joy. Everyone instantly saw the difference in Edwin, Theodore especially. Brenna prayed it would open their eyes.

Brenna gave Benjamin a quick hug. He was already warming up to her.

"Well, I say we return home. I need to make up all the time I've missed, namely a certain grandson of mine.

"That sounds lovely," Brenna smiled.

CHAPTER THIRTY-FOUR

hey remained in London for a week. Since they were there, they made a quick visit to Bertram and Adelaide's then prepared to board a ship back to Ireland. Again they found themselves on the busy harbor, getting their luggage into the ship.

Brenna marveled at the goodness of God as she patiently waited. She gazed up at the sunny blue sky, almost in the same spot as when they came. When they arrived in England at the beginning of July, she was hoping and praying they would find her family.

And now my entire family has been restored back to me. Lord, You are so good! You are the God of more than enough...making impossible things possible, Brenna silently rejoiced.

"Dear, could you assist me with where you would like to put some of these things?" Rylan called to her. Brenna, who was holding Breckin, placed him back in the buggy that her father held onto.

"I'll be right back."

"Don't worry about us. We'll be just fine, won't we?" William's voice grew higher as he leaned over the buggy. Breckin began to fuss when Brenna left so William decided to walk him. He was quite taken with his first grandchild. In fact, he barely left him.

"Well, who is this little prince?" William came to a halt and glanced up to see who had said it and found a short, older woman. She had been walking along and must have heard the baby fussing. William still pushed the buggy back and forth to quiet him. He couldn't think of the particulars but he knew he'd seen the lady somewhere before. She gazed into the buggy and smiled sweetly.

"This is my grandson," he stated proudly.

"Ah, I can clock the resemblance." William chuckled at this.

Brenna finished up with the servants and went to go and get her father. When she found him up the street a little ways, talking to someone, she went to him and overheard the woman.

"Wot is the golden dove's name?"

What did she say? Brenna's heart quickened at the strangely familiar words. She was nearly upon them when William replied.

"His name is Breckin."

"Is that so? What a jubly lush— " the woman stopped in mid-sentence, looked up, and met Brenna's gaze just as she walked up behind William. Brenna couldn't believe her eyes at

who it appeared to be.
　　"Hephzibah!"

"Who being the brightness of his glory, and the express image of his person, and upholding all things by the word of his power, when he had by himself purged our sins, sat down on the right hand of the Majesty on high."

Hebrews 1:3

Kelly Aul

Kelly Aul lives in a small, rural town in Minnesota with her parents and two younger siblings. They were homeschooled which made their family very close. Growing up, Kelly had a very vivid imagination. She was always pretending, making up games with her siblings, and finding adventure around her home on a small lake. Kelly is enthralled with European history, especially the 19th century, writing, and most importantly the things of God. She is in full time ministry, along with her family, studying to be a pastor. She also works part time as a pharmacy technician.

Some people might be thinking, "Why do you have to mention God throughout this whole book? Dedication and everything?"

"Whatsoever ye do in word or deed, do all in the name of the Lord Jesus." (Colossians 3:17)

I can't stop talking about Him because He *is* my everything. And because He's my everything, God is in everything I do.

I've read some Christian novels and it seems almost as if they try to go as close to the edge as they can and still call it a Christian book, but the question shouldn't be how close can I get before crossing the line. It should be, how close can I get to God? How much can I talk about Him? How can I give more glory to Him?

I don't ever want my readers to have to ask themselves, "Should I be reading this? Would God read this book? Could I read this book in front of my pastor or parents without guilt?"

Thank you for reading. I hope you enjoyed yourself and were inspired. And I have to say again, I give God all the glory for every part of this book. Without Him, I can do nothing.

— God bless, Kelly

Jesus said, except a man be born again, he cannot see the kingdom of God. (John 3:3) Being born again or the New Birth is not: confirmation, church membership, water baptism, being moral, doing good deeds.

Ephesians 2:8-9 "For by grace are ye saved through faith; and that not of yourselves: it is the gift of God: not of works, lest any man should boast."

You have to simply admit you are just what the Bible says — a lost sinner. Then you come and accept what Christ has purchased for you — a gift! (Romans 10:9-10)

Please pray this prayer to receive Jesus as your Savior.

Dear Heavenly Father, I believe in my heart that Jesus Christ is the son of God, that He was crucified, died, and rose from the dead.

I ask you, Lord Jesus, to be Lord of my life. Thank you for saving me and coming into my heart, for forgiving me and redeeming me from all sin.

It's important to find a church where they teach the Word of God by studying right from the Bible, and to renew your mind by reading the Bible every day.

— Maggie Aul, Senior Pastor
Love of God Family Church
www.LoveofGodFamilyChurch.com

Kelly Aul

Spoiler Alert!

The Author recommends readers not to read beyond this point
until they finish reading this book, Holding Faith.
There's nothing worse than ruining the mystery in the pages!

Family Tree

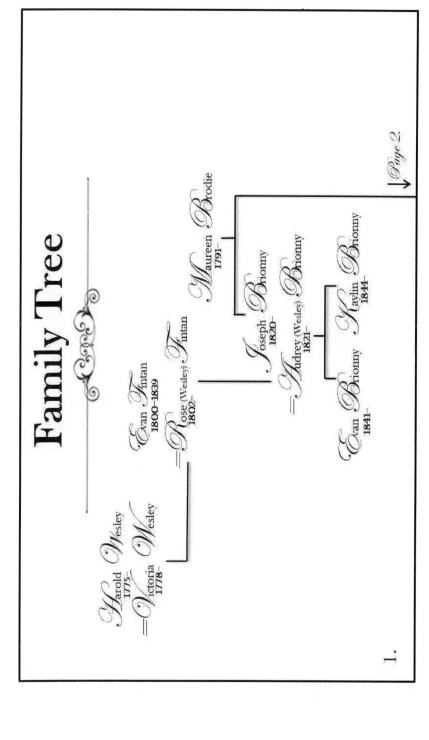

Harold *Wesley*
1775–
= Victoria *Wesley*
1778–

Evan *Fintan*
1800–1839
= Rose (Wesley) *Fintan*
1802–

Maureen *Brodie*
1791–

Joseph *Brionny*
1820–
= Audrey (Wesley) *Brionny*
1821–

Evan *Brionny*
1841–

Kaylin *Brionny*
1841–

→ *Page 2.*

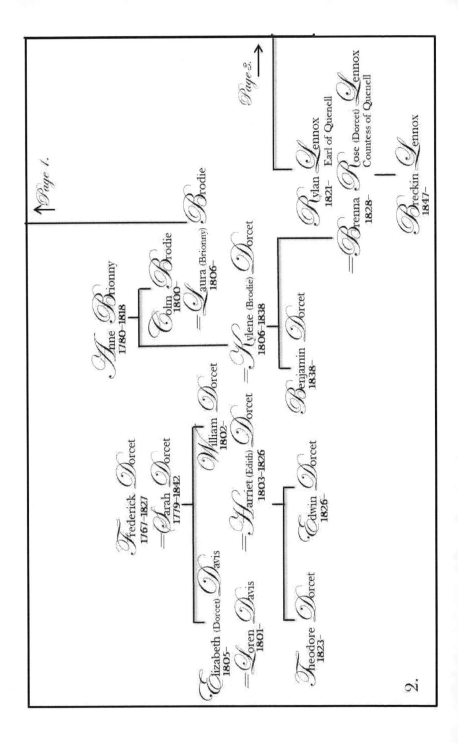

←Page 1.

Page 3.→

Anne Brionny
1780-1818

Brodie

Colm Brodie
1800

=*Laura (Brionny)*
1806-

Frederick Dorcet
1767-1827

=*Sarah Dorcet*
1779-1842

William Dorcet
1802-

=*Harriet (Edith) Dorcet*
1803-1826

=*Kylene (Brodie) Dorcet*
1806-1838

Benjamin Dorcet
1838-

Rylan Lennox
Earl of Quenell
1821-

=*Rose (Dorcet) Lennox*
Countess of Quenell
1828-

Brenna Lennox

Breckin Lennox
1847-

Elizabeth (Dorcet) Davis
1805-

=*Loren Davis*
1801-

Edwin Dorcet
1826-

Theodore Dorcet
1823-

2.

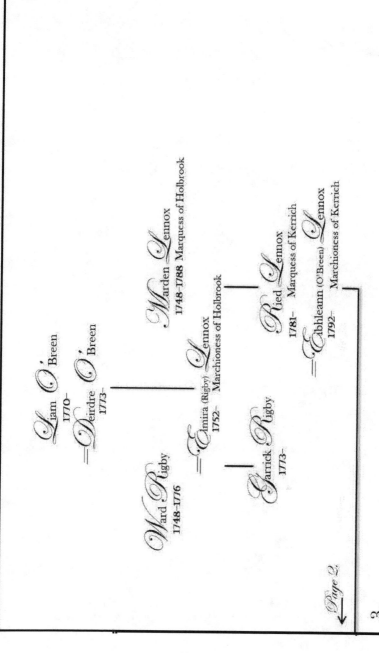

Liam O'Breen
1770–
Deirdre O'Breen
1773–

Ward Rigby
1748-1776

Warden Lennox
1748-1788 Marquess of Holbrook

Elmira (Rigby) Lennox
1752– Marchioness of Holbrook

Garrick Rigby
1773–

Ried Lennox
1781– Marquess of Kerrich

Eibhleann (O'Breen) Lennox
1792– Marchioness of Kerrich

Page 2.

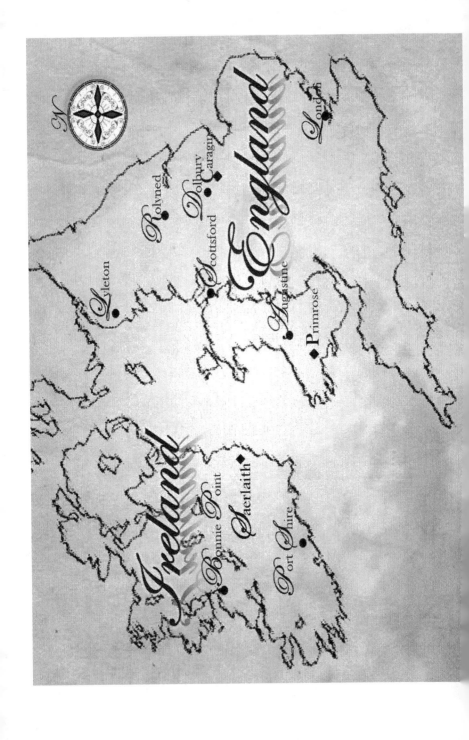

1772		John McNiel born
1800		Colm Brodie born
1804		John McNiel marries Lenora
1805		John and Lenora McNiel have son, Dennon
1806		Kylene Brodie Born
		Laura Brionny born
		Reid Lennox (Marquess of Kerrich) marries Eibhleann O'Breen
1808		Lenora McNiel goes to America with Dennon
		John McNiel goes after his wife and son once he saved enough money
		Dennon McNiel dies
1810		Maureen Brionny has miscarriage
1814		John McNiel gets a job with Princeton Shipping Company and eventually becomes Captain
1815		Maureen Brionny has son
1816		Maureen Brionny's son dies
1818		Colm and Kylene Brodie's Parents Die. They move to America
		Captain McNiel finds Pete (Lenora's Brother) and almost kills him - instead, Pete shoots McNiel in the leg
1820		Joseph Brionny born
	April	Willian Dorcet meets Kylene Brodie
	August	Captain McNiel throws Evan and Rose Fintan off of his ship, The St. Carlin
1821		Rylan Lennox born

1821		Audrey Wesley born
	August	Frederick Dorcet finds out about William's secret relationship with Kylene and breaks them apart.
	October	William marries Harriet Edith
1823		William and Harriet have a son, Theodore Dorcet
1826		William and Harriet have a son, Edwin Dorcet
	May	Frederich Dorcet has heart attack
	July	Harriet Dorcet dies
1827	May	Frederick Dorcet dies
		Colm Brodie is offered job in Ireland after his uncle dies. Colm and Kylene plan to return to Ireland
	August	William finds and marries Kylene Brodie - Colm goes to Ireland alone
1828		Brenna Rose Dorcet born
1833		Man comes to buy Brionny land
		Joseph Brionny's father dies
		Famine comes to Ireland and Joseph gets a job on ship
1834		Colm Brodie marries Laura Brionny
1835	March	Brionny's house is started on fire with Maureen and Laura inside
1838	June	Joseph Brionny comes home and thinks his family died in fire
	August	Joseph gets a job on The St. Carlin
	November	William and Kylene have a son, Benjamin Dorcet

1839		After searching for the shell for eighteen years, Captain McNiel kidnapps Audrey Wesley
		Joseph Brionny meets Audrey Wesley
	July	Captain McNiel dies in storm
	August	Brenna gets to London, England
	September	Audrey comes home
		Lanna Ryan goes to Cheverell's for The London Season
	November	Lanna meets Stephen Kinsey
1840	July	Joseph Brionny marries Audrey Wesley
1841	June	Joseph and Audrey have a son, Evan Brionny
	October	Stephen and Lanna have a son, Tully Kinsey
1842		Stephen and Lanna take in Brenna Dorcet
		Stephen and Lanna have a daughter, Audrey Kinsey
1844	April	Joseph and Audrey have a daughter, Kalin Brionny
	May	Brenna meets Rylan Lennox, Earl of Quenell
	July	Jake Harper marries Rose Wesley
1845	March	Rylan marries Brenna
	May	Brenna has dream about wheat
	August	The Blight
1846	August	The second Blight
1847	May	Rylan and Brenna have a son, Breckin Lennox
	June	Joseph Brionny finds his mother and sister
		Brenna finds her family

❖ Pronunciation of Eibhleann ~ Avelynn

❖ Pronunciation of Saerlaith ~ ser-la

Never Forsaken ~ Book One

She knows nothing of the tragedy that haunts her family's past.

Audrey has had enough of the emptiness of society and prays for something more. Unbeknown to her, someone is watching her every move just waiting for the right moment. It's only when Audrey faces death that her faith proves true at all costs in the midst of the storm. A new beginning is finally able to transpire when all is revealed and love is found in the most unlikely place.

AUDREY'S SUNRISE BOOK PREVIEW
Check out the video!
http://youtu.be/mrgABZLImjc

Never Forsaken ~ Book Two

She is held captive within herself with no chance of being rescued.

One decision changed their family forever. One choice tore them apart. Their every thought is now consumed with regret.

When everything she holds dear is taken away, her faith dwindles to nothing. She has no choice but to resign herself to the sorrowful fact that her once childlike faith in God, was nothing more than that...childish.

It isn't long before something else discovers her vulnerable state. She doesn't know what it is until it's too late. There is no one to turn to and the dreadful grips of fear, that haunts her every move, is hers alone to endure.

Try as she might to hide away her past completely, her persistent dreams won't let her forget. She's tempted to give in to the black shadows and simply give up.

She soon finds herself desperately searching for the one place she never wanted to see again. It is where she comes upon a treasure. Something that holds her only rescue from the dark presence pursuing her, as she finds hope in the midst of darkness.

IN THE MIDST OF DARKNESS BOOK PREVIEW
Check out the video!

http://youtu.be/0FeHG-E06OQ

Never Forsaken ~ Book Four

He found a love so great, it was stronger than death itself.

When the one person Reid looked up to the most was stolen from him, a single promise gave him the determination needed to go on. Reid continually fights against every possible hindrance and rejection from high society. A relationship that should have brought joy, was built upon nothing more than secrets and deception. The love he'd sought after had betrayed him. Reid didn't know who he could trust, other than himself. That is until the unthinkable happens and leaves him completely helpless. Reid was forced to examine his life and it was then that he was shown a love so vast, he realized this unconditional love only comes from God. Little did her know what would be required of him. To lay down his life for another. A brother's hatred, a son's promise, and the Father's everlasting love would change the course of a rejected people forever.

EVERLASTING BOOK PREVIEW
Check out the video!

https://youtu.be/VATXE3_yQpw

Available online:

www.amazon.com

www.barnesandnoble.com

www.kobobooks.com

(Also for eBooks!)

Available in stores:

Trumm Drug in Elbow Lake, MN

Higher Grounds in Fergus Falls, MN

❖ Please visit the Official Author Website

www.kellyaul.com

❖ Like on Facebook

facebook.com/KellyAulNovels

88803768R00143

Made in the USA
Columbia, SC
11 February 2018